Philip Schaff

Saint Augustin

Three Biographies

Philip Schaff

Saint Augustin
Three Biographies

ISBN/EAN: 9783337340964

Printed in Europe, USA, Canada, Australia, Japan

Cover: Foto ©Raphael Reischuk / pixelio.de

More available books at **www.hansebooks.com**

Three Biographies.

BY

PHILIP SCHAFF, D.D.

AUTHOR OF

"THROUGH BIBLE LANDS," "THE PERSON OF CHRIST,"
"CHRIST AND CHRISTIANITY," ETC.

LONDON:

JAMES NISBET & CO., 21 BERNERS STREET.

MDCCCLXXXVI.

TO

𝔐𝔶 𝔅𝔢𝔩𝔬𝔳𝔢𝔡 𝔖𝔱𝔲𝔡𝔢𝔫𝔱𝔰

I DEDICATE THESE BIOGRAPHICAL SKETCHES OF

ST. AUGUSTIN, MELANCHTHON, AND NEANDER,

THE CHURCH FATHER, THE REFORMER, AND

THE CHURCH HISTORIAN,

THREE OF THE BEST AMONG THE GREAT, AND OF THE

GREATEST AMONG THE GOOD,

WITNESSES OF THE UNITY OF THE SPIRIT IN THE DIVERSITIES

OF GIFTS,

AND AS INSPIRING EXAMPLES OF CONSECRATION TO THE

SERVICE OF CHRIST.

PHILIP SCHAFF.

UNION THEOLOGICAL SEMINARY,
NEW YORK, *December* 1885.

CONTENTS.

SAINT AUGUSTIN.

MELANCHTHON.

REMINISCENCES OF NEANDER.

SAINT AUGUSTIN.

INTRODUCTORY.

THE chief, almost the only source of the life of St. Augustin till the time of his conversion is his autobiography; his faithful friend, Possidius, added a few notices; his public labors till his death are recorded in his numerous writings; his influence is written on the pages of mediæval and modern church history.

Among religious autobiographies the *Confessions* of Augustin still hold the first rank. In them this remarkable man, endowed with a lofty genius and a burning heart, lays open his inner life before God and the world, and at the same time the life of God in his own soul, which struggled for the mastery, and at last obtained it. A more honest book was never written. He conceals nothing, he palliates nothing. Like a faithful witness against himself, standing at the bar of the omniscient Judge, he tells the truth, the whole truth, and nothing but the truth. Like King David, in the fifty-first Psalm, he openly confesses his transgressions with unfeigned sorrow and grief, yet in the joyous consciousness of forgiveness. To his sense of sin corresponds his sense of grace: they are the controlling ideas of his spiritual life and of his system of theology. The deeper the descent into the hell of self-knowledge, the higher the ascent to the knowledge of God.

Augustin might have kept the secret of his youthful aberrations; posterity knows them only from his pen.

He committed no murder nor adultery, like the King of Israel ; he never denied his Saviour, like Peter ; he was no persecutor of the Church, like Paul ; his sins preceded his conversion and baptism, and they were compatible with the highest honor in heathen society. But his Christian experience quickened his sense of guilt, and he told the story for his own humiliation and for the glory of God's redeeming grace.

The *Confessions* are a solemn soliloquy before the throne of the Searcher of hearts within the hearing of the world. They enter into the deepest recesses of religious experience, and rise to the lofty summit of theological thought. They exhibit a mind intensely pious and at the same time intensely speculative. His prayers are meditations, and his meditations are prayers ; and both shine and burn like Africa's tropical sun. They reflect, as Guizot says, " a unique mixture of passion and gentleness, of authority and sympathy, of largeness of mind and logical rigor." Dr. Shedd ranks them among those rare autobiographies in which " the ordinary experiences of human life attain to such a pitch of intensity and such a breadth, range, and depth as to strike the reader with both a sense of familiarity and a sense of strangeness. It is his own human thought and human feeling that he finds expressed ; and yet it is spoken with so much greater clearness, depth, and energy than he is himself capable of, or than is characteristic of the mass of men, that it seems like the experience of another sphere and another race of beings." *

Even in a psychological and literary point of view the *Confessions* of Augustin rank among the most interest-

---

* See the thoughtful introduction to his edition of the *Confessions of Augustin*, Andover, 1860, p. ix.

ing of autobiographies, and are not inferior to Rousseau's
Confessions and Goethe's *Truth and Fiction;* while in
religious value there is no comparison between them.
They are equally frank, and blend the personal with the
general human interest; but while the French philosopher and the German poet are absorbed in the analysis
of their own self, and dwell upon it with satisfaction, the
African father goes into the minute details of his sins
and follies with intense abhorrence of sin, and rises
above himself to the contemplation of divine mercy,
which delivered him from the degrading slavery. The
former wrote for the glory of man, the latter for the
glory of God. Augustin lived in an age when the Western Roman Empire was fast approaching dissolution, and
the Christian Church, the true City of God, was being
built on its ruins. He was not free from the defects of
an artificial and degenerate rhetoric; nevertheless he
rises not seldom to the height of passionate eloquence,
and scatters gems of the rarest beauty. He was master
of the antithetical power, the majesty and melody of the
language of imperial Rome. Many of his sentences have
passed into proverbial use, and become commonplaces in
theological literature.

Next to Augustin himself, his mother attracts the
attention and excites the sympathy of the reader. She
walks like a guardian angel from heaven through his
book until her translation to that sphere. How pure and
strong and enduring her devotion to him, and his devotion to her! She dried many tears of anxious mothers.
It is impossible to read of Monnica without a profounder
regard for woman and a feeling of gratitude for Christianity, which raised her to so high a position.

The *Confessions* were written about A.D. 397, ten
years after Augustin's conversion. The historical part

closes with his conversion and with the death of his mother. The work contains much that can be fully understood only by the theologian and the student of history ; and the last four of the thirteen books are devoted to subtle speculations about the nature of memory, eternity, time, and creation, which far transcend the grasp of the ordinary reader. Nevertheless it was read with great interest and profit in the time of the writer, and ever since, in the original Latin and numerous translations in various languages. In all that belongs to elevation, depth, and emotion there are few books so edifying and inspiring and so well worthy of careful study as Augustin's *Confessions.*

We shall endeavor to popularize the *Confessions,* and to supplement the biography from other sources, for the instruction and edification of the present generation. The life of a great genius and saint like Augustin is one of the best arguments for the religion he professed, and to which he devoted his mental and moral energies.

CHAPTER I.

AURELIUS AUGUSTINUS, the greatest and best, and the most influential of the Latin church-fathers, was born on the thirteenth of November, 354, at Tagaste, in Numidia, North Africa. His birthplace was near Hippo Regius (now Bona), where he spent his public life as presbyter and bishop, and where he died in the seventy-sixth year of his age (Aug. 28, 430). He belonged to the Punic race, which was of Phœnician origin, but became Latinized in language, laws, and customs under Roman rule since the destruction of Carthage (b.c. 146), yet retained the Oriental temper and the sparks of the genius of Hannibal, the sworn enemy of Rome. These traits appear in the writings of Tertullian and Cyprian, who preceded Augustin and prepared the way for his theology. In Augustin we can trace the religious intensity of the Semitic race, the tropical fervor of Africa, the Catholic grasp and comprehensiveness of Rome, and the germs of an evangelical revolt against its towering ambition and tyrannical rule. His native land has long since been laid waste by the barbarous Vandals (A.D. 439) and the Mohammedan Arabs (647), and keeps mournful silence over dreary ruins; but his spirit marched through the ages, and still lives and acts as a molding and stimulating power in all the branches of Western Christendom.

His father, Patricius, was a member of the city Council, and a man of kindly disposition, but irritable temper and dissolute habits. He remained a heathen till shortly before his death, but did not, as it appears, lay any obstruction to the Christian course of his wife.

Monnica,* the mother of Augustin, shines among the most noble and pious women that adorn the grand temple of the Christian Church. She was born in the year 331 or 332, of Christian parents, probably at Tagaste. She had rare gifts of mind and heart, which were developed by an excellent Christian education, and dedicated to the Saviour. To the violent passion of her husband she opposed an angelic meekness, and when the outburst was over she reproached him so tenderly that he was always shamed. Had the rebuke been administered sooner it would only have fed the unhallowed fire. His conjugal infidelity she bore with patience and forgiving love. Her highest aim was to win him over to the Christian faith—not so much by words as by a truly humble and godly conduct and the conscientious discharge of her household duties. In this she was so successful that, a year before his death, he enrolled himself among the catechumens and was baptized. To her it was the greatest pleasure to read the Holy Scriptures

---

* This is the correct spelling, according to the oldest MSS. of the writings of Augustin, and is followed by Pusey, in his edition of the *Confessions,* by Moule, in Smith and Wace, *Dict. of Christian Biography,* III. 932, and also by K. Braune, in *Monnika und Augustinus* (Grimma, 1846). The usual spelling is *Monica,* in French *Monique.* It is derived by some from μόνος, *single;* by others from μόννος or μάννος, Lat. *monile, a necklace (monilia, jewels).*

and to attend church regularly every morning and evening, "not," as Augustin says, "to listen to vain fables,
but to the Lord, in the preaching of His servants, and to
offer up to Him her prayers." She esteemed it a precious privilege to lay on the altar each day a gift of love,
to bestow alms on the poor, and to extend hospitality to
strangers, especially to brethren in the faith. She
brought up her children in the nurture and admonition
of the Lord. She bare Augustin, as he boasts of her,
with greater pains spiritually than she had brought him
forth naturally into the world.* For thirty years she
prayed for the conversion of her distinguished son, until
at last, a short time before her death, after manifold
cares and burning tears, in the midst of which she never
either murmured against God or lost hope, she found
her prayers answered beyond her expectations. She has
become a bright example and rich comfort for mothers,
and will act as an inspiration to the end of time.

From such parents sprang Augustin. Strong sensual
passions he inherited from his father, but from his
mother those excellent gifts of mind and heart which,
though long perverted, were at last reclaimed by the
regenerating grace of God, and converted into an incal-
culable blessing to the Church of all ages. He had a
brother, by the name of Navigius, a widowed sister,
who presided over a society of pious women till the day
of her death, and a number of nephews and nieces.

Augustin says that with his mother's milk his heart
sucked in the name of the Saviour, which became so

---

* *Confess.* 1. V. c. 9 : "*Non enim satis eloquor, quid erga me habebat
animi, et quanto majore sollicitudine me parturiebat spiritu, quam carne
perpererat.*" Likewise 1. IX. c. 8 : "*Quæ me parturivit, et carne, ut
in hanc temporalem, et corde, ut in æternam lucem nascerer.*" Comp. his
whole description of Monnica, ix. 9–12.

firmly lodged there that nothing which did not savor of
that name, however learned and attractive it might otherwise be, could ever fully charm him. He early lisped
out prayers to God, whose all-embracing love revealed
itself to his childish spirit. These germs of piety were
overgrown by the weeds of youthful vice and impure
lusts, but never wholly smothered. Even in the midst
of his furthest wanderings he still heard the low, sad
echo of his youthful religious impressions, was attended
by the guardian genius of his praying mother, and felt
in the depths of his noble spirit the pulse-beat of that
strong desire after God, to which, in the opening of
his *Confessions*, he gives utterance in the incompar-
able words : " Thou, O God, hast created us for Thyself, and our heart is without rest, until it rests in
Thee." *

He was not baptized in infancy, but merely offered to
the initiation of a catechumen by the sign of the cross
and the salting with salt.† There was at that time no
compulsory baptism of infants : it was left to the free
choice of the parents. Monnica probably shared the
view of Tertullian that it was safer to postpone baptism
to years of discretion than to run the risk of forfeiting
its benefit by a relapse.

Augustin was sent to school at an early age, with the
hope on the part of his father that he might become distinguished in the world ; on that of his mother, that

---

* *Confess.* I. 1 : "*Fecisti nos ad Te, et inquietum est cor nostrum, donec
requiescat in Te.*" Dr. Pusey, in his translation (based on an older
one), obliterates the paronomasia—*inquietum, requiescat* : " Thou
madest us for Thyself, and our heart is *restless*, until it *repose* in
Thee." Dr. Shedd retains this translation.

† *Confess.* I. 11.

"the common studies might not only prove innocent, but also in some degree useful in leading him afterward to God."

Elementary instruction and mathematics were, however, too dry for the boy; and he was, in consequence, severely punished by his teachers. Play was his chief delight. In order to shine as the first among his companions he even cheated them; and for the purpose of providing himself with playthings, or of gratifying his appetite, he went so far as to steal from the store-room and the table of his parents. At public shows he passionately crowded himself into the front ranks of the spectators.

And yet for all this he had to endure the reproaches of conscience. On one occasion, when, seized by a violent cramp in the stomach, he believed his last hour had come, he earnestly begged to be baptized. But after his mother had made the necessary preparations he suddenly grew better, and the baptism, according to a prevailing notion of the age, was postponed, lest this precious means for the washing away of past sins might be rendered vain by the contraction of new guilt, in which case no other remedy was to be found. At a later period he thought it would have been far better for him had he been early received by baptism into the communion of the Church, and thus placed under her protecting care.

His dislike for learning ceased when Augustin passed over from rudimentary studies into the grammar school. The poet Vergil charmed his fancy and filled him with fresh enthusiasm. With the deepest interest he followed Æneas in his wanderings, and shed tears over the death of Dido, who slew herself for love; while at the same time, as he tells us, he ought to have mourned over his own

death in estrangement from God.* The wooden horse
full of armed warriors, the burning of Troy, and the
shade of Creusa were continually before his soul. The
Grecian classics were not so much to his taste, because
his defective knowledge of the language, which he never
had the patience to master, prevented the enjoyment of
their works.

By his gift of lively representation and brilliant orator-
ical talent he made a figure in the school, and awakened
the fondest hopes in the hearts of his parents. His
father destined him to the then highly respectable and
influential office of rhetorician, or public teacher of
forensic eloquence. For further improvement he sent
him to the larger neighboring city of Madaura, where
heathenism still held almost exclusive sway. His residence there was probably injurious to him in a moral
point of view.

In the sixteenth year of his age he returned home in
order to prepare himself, in as cheap a manner as possible, for the University of the metropolis of Northern
Africa. But instead of growing better he entered upon
the path of folly, and plunged into the excesses of sensuality. His mother earnestly exhorted him to lead a
chaste life ; but he was ashamed to heed the exhortation
of a woman. This false shame drove him even to pre-
tend frequently to crimes which he had never committed, so as not to seem to fall behind his comrades. He
himself confesses, " I was not able to distinguish the
brighter purity of love from the darkness of lust. Both

---

* *Confess.* I. 13 : " *Quid enim miserius misero non miserante seipsum,*
et flente Didonis mortem, quæ fiebat amando Æneam ; non flente autem
mortem suam, quæ fiebat non amando Te, Deus lumen cordis mei, et
panis oris intus animæ meæ, et virtus maritans mentem meam, et sinum
cogitationis meæ ?"

were mingled together in confusion ; youth in its weakness, hurried to the abyss of desire, was swallowed up in the pool of vice."

Yet, amid these wild impulses, it was not well with him. That longing after God, so deeply rooted in his soul, asserted its power again and again. He became more and more discontented with himself, and after every indulgence felt an inward pang. The guiding hand of the Lord mixed in the cup of his enjoyment " the wholesome bitterness that leads us back from destructive pleasure, by which we are estranged from God."

CHAPTER II.

AUGUSTIN AT CARTHAGE.

In his seventeenth year, the same in which his father died, he entered the High School of Carthage, supported by his mother and the richest citizen of Tagaste, Romanianus, who was a distant relative. Carthage was the Rome of Africa, with many marble palaces, numerous schools, countless shows, and shameless vices. Monnica did not see her son depart for the great and voluptuous city without fear and trembling, but she was not willing now to interrupt his career, and she knew Him who is stronger than all temptation, and listens to the prayers of His children. In Carthage Augustin studied oratory and other sciences, astrology even, and raised himself to the first rank by his talent. This increased his ambition and fed his pride.

With his morals he fared badly. He consorted with a

B

class of students who sought their honor in deriding good conduct, and called themselves " Destroyers." Although their rough and vulgar doings were peculiarly disagreeable to a nature so noble as his, yet their society must have exerted over him a pernicious influence. He frequently visited also the tragic theatre, because it was always, says he, " filled with pictures of my misery, and tinder for my desires."

In his eighteenth year he took up with a woman, with whom he lived thirteen years without marriage, and was faithful to her. She bore him a son, Adeodatus, whose promising gifts gave his father much joy, but he died at an early age. She walks veiled through the *Confessions*, a memory without a name, and disappears with a sigh of repentance and a vow to devote herself to a pure and single life.

It should be borne in mind that the excesses of his youth are known to us only from his own honest *Confessions*. His worst sin was common in the best heathen society, and sanctioned by the Roman law. It did not in the least affect his respectability in the eyes of the world. Even the Emperor Marcus Aurelius, the model saint and philosopher of ancient Rome, kept a concubine after the death of his wife, without feeling the least scruple. Tertullian, Cyprian, Jerome, and other eminent fathers who embraced Christianity in adult years, were probably no better than Augustin before his conversion, but they left only vague allusions. Augustin never was a profligate. He was strictly faithful to the one woman of his affection, the first from Africa, the second from Italy.* It is therefore an inexcusable slander to call him " the

---

* *Confess.* IV. 2 : "*In illis annis unam habebam*, . . *sed unam tamen, ci quoque servans tori fidem.*" Comp. VI. 15.

promiscuous lover of the frail beauties of Carthage."
It was wicked and brutal in Byron to write that Saint
Augustin's "fine *Confessions* make the reader envy his
transgressions." The wisdom of some parts of his *Confessions* may be doubted, but they were made to impress
the reader with his own intense abhorrence of sin, and
we must admire the fearless honesty and keen moral
sensibility of the man in revealing the secrets of his
former life, which otherwise would never have been
known.

CHAPTER III.

CICERO'S HORTENSIUS.

MEANWHILE, beneath this rushing stream of external
activity, the soul of Augustin sighed after true wisdom.
His ardent thirst for something ideal and enduring first
of all showed itself in the study of the *Hortensius* of
Cicero, which came up regularly in the course of his
education. This lost volume contained an encouragement to true philosophy, and gave the direction, in its
study, to aim at truth only, and, above all, to hail her
footsteps with enthusiasm and without regard to the interest of party. This roused the young man to an earnest struggle after truth.

"This book," says he, "transformed my inclinations
and turned my prayers to Thee, O God, and changed
my wishes and my desires. Every vain hope was ex-
tinguished; and I longed, with an incredible fervor of
spirit, after the immortality of wisdom. I began to raise
myself that I might return to Thee. I studied this book

again and again, not for the refinement of my language nor for aid in the art of speaking, but in order that I might be persuaded by its doctrine. Oh, how I burned, my God—how I burned to fly back from the things of earth to Thee. And I knew not what Thou hadst designed with me. For with Thee is wisdom, and these writings excited me toward love, toward wisdom, toward philosophy. And this particularly delighted me, that I was not asked therein to love, to seek, to attain, and to hold in firm embrace this or that school—but wisdom alone, as she might reveal herself. I was charmed and inflamed."

But the volume contained one blemish : the name of Christ was not there. Such a secret power did that name, imprinted on his tender soul, exert over him, even during his wanderings.

In this thirst after truth he laid hold of the records of revelation—that holy book to which his mother clung with such reverent devotion. But there was yet a great gulf fixed between him and the Bible. In order to be understood it requires an humble, childlike disposition. To the proud in spirit it is a book with seven seals. The natural man perceives not the things that belong to the Spirit of God : they are foolishness unto him, because they are spiritually discerned. Augustin was not yet acquainted with the depth of his corruption, which the Holy Scriptures disclosed to him on every page. "The Scriptures," he says, "thrive among the childlike ; but I refused to become a child, and thought myself great in my own presumption." He desired not truth in her simple beauty, but arrayed in a specious garb of rhetoric, to flatter his vanity ; he desired her not as a chaste virgin, but as a voluptuous courtesan.

Hence he now turned to the sect of the Manichæans,

who had the word truth always on their lips, but held their disciples captive in the bondage of error.

CHAPTER IV.

AUGUSTIN AMONG THE MANICHÆANS.

The Manichæans, so called from their founder, the Persian Mani, or Manichæus (died 274), were a sect allied to the Gnostics. They blended together heathenism and Christianity in a fantastic system, which they set up in opposition to Judaism and the Catholic Church. The groundwork of their doctrine is the Old Persian religion, into which a few Christian elements are introduced in a distorted form. They were dualists; they taught, as Zoroaster, an original antagonism between God and matter; between the kingdom of light and the kingdom of darkness; between good and evil. Man stands in the middle between both these kingdoms; he has a spark of light in him which longs after redemption, but, at the same time, is possessed of a corrupt body and a corrupt soul, which are to be gradually annihilated. To a certain degree they acknowledged Christ as a Saviour, but confounded Him with the sun; for they were accustomed to drag down the spiritual ideas of the gospel into the sphere of natural life. In the entire economy of nature, which, along with the perfume of the flower, sends the miasmatic breath, and causes the gloomy night to succeed the clear day, they saw a conflict between the two opposite kingdoms; in every plant a crucified Christ, an imprisoned spirit of light, which

worked itself up from the dark bosom of the earth and
strove toward the sun.   The class of the *perfect* among
them durst slay or wound no animal, pluck no flower,
break no stalk of grass, for fear of injuring the higher
spirit dwelling in it.   They regarded the whole Catholic
Church as contaminated by Judaistic elements.   Mani is
the Paraclete or Advocate promised by Christ, who is to
restore again the true Church.   They reproached the
orthodox Christians for believing blindly, on mere
authority, and for not elevating themselves to the standpoint of independent knowledge.   They, the Manichæans, thought themselves, on the contrary, in the possession of perfect knowledge, of truth in her pure, unveiled
form.   The words truth, science, reason, never out of
their mouths, were esteemed as excellent baits for strangers.

These lofty pretensions and promises to unravel all the
riddles of existence, the longing after redemption, characteristic of the system, its inward sympathy with the
life of nature, the dazzling show of its subtle dialectics
and polemics against the doctrines of the church, and the
ascetic severity of its course of life, explain the attractive
power which the Manichæan philosophy exerted over
many of the more profound spirits of the age, and the
extensive propagation which it met with even in the
West.

We can readily imagine how Augustin, taken up with
his struggles after truth, but at the same time full of intellectual pride, as he then was, should be won over by
its delusive charms.   He enrolled himself in the class of
the *auditors*, or catechumens.   His mother mourned
over this new aberration, but was consoled by a dream,
in which a shining youth told her that her son should
stand just where she stood.   When she informed her son

of it, he interpreted the dream as implying the speedy conversion of his mother to his side. " No, no," answered she, " it was not said to me, where he is there shalt thou be also ; but, where thou art, there shall he be also." Augustin confesses that this prompt reply made a greater impression on him than the dream itself. She was likewise comforted by a bishop, who, at a former period, had been himself a Manichæan. She begged him to convince her son of his error. But he thought disputation would be of no avail. She should only continue to pray for him, and gradually, of his own accord, through study and experience, he would come to a clearer understanding. " As sure as you live," he added, " it is not possible that a son of such tears should be lost." Monnica treasured up these words as a prophetic voice from heaven.

For nine years, up to the twenty-eighth of his life, Augustin remained in connection with these heretics— led astray, and leading others astray. Their discovery of seeming contradictions in the doctrines of the Church, their polemics against the Old Testament, their speculations concerning the origin of evil, which they traced back to a primordial principle co-existent with God Himself, spoke to his understanding, while their symbolical interpretations of the varied aspects of nature addressed his lively imagination.

And yet, for all this, the deepest want of his reason remained unsatisfied. At the time of the high church festivals particularly, when all Christians flocked to the services of the altar, in order to die with the Lord on Good Friday, and rise again with Him on Easter morning, he was seized with a strong desire after their communion. For this reason he took no step toward entering the higher class of the initiated, or *elect*, among the

Manichæans, but devoted himself more zealously to those studies which belonged to his calling as a rhetorician.

CHAPTER V.

THE LOSS OF A FRIEND.

AFTER the completion of his course of study he returned to Tagaste, in order to settle there as a teacher of rhetoric. He was master of every qualification for inspiring his scholars with enthusiasm, and many of them, especially Alypius, adhered to him through life with the most heartfelt gratitude.

About this time he lost a very dear friend, who, with an almost feminine susceptibility, had resigned himself to the commanding power of his creative intellect, and had even followed him into the mazes of Manichæism. He was suddenly prostrated by a fever. Baptism was administered to him without his knowledge; Augustin, who was with him night and day, made a mock of it. But his friend, when he again became conscious, withstood him with an independence that he had never before exhibited. The empty shadow of a Christ, the sun, the moon, the air, and whatever else was pointed out by Manichæism to the soul thirsting after salvation, could now yield him no comfort—but the simple, childlike faith of the Catholic Church alone. In this faith he departed, when the fever returned with renewed violence.

The death of this friend filled Augustin with inexpressible anguish. Neither the splendor of light, nor the peaceful innocence of the flowers, nor the joys of the banquet, nor the pleasures of sense, had any interest for him now ; even his books, for a long while, lost their charms. "Everything I looked upon was death. My fatherland became a torment to me—my father's house a scene of the deepest suffering. Above all, my eyes sought after him ; but he was not given back to me again. I hated everything because he was not there. I had become a great enigma to myself."

He afterward saw how wrong it was to place such unbounded dependence on the creature. "Oh, the folly," he laments, "of not knowing how to love men as men ! Oh, foolish man, to suffer what is human beyond due measure, as I then did !" "Blessed is he, O Lord, who loves Thee," are his inimitable words, "and his friend in Thee, and his enemy for Thy sake. He alone loses no dear ones, to whom all are dear in Him, who can never be lost to us. And who is He, but our God, the God who made heaven and earth, and fills them all ! No one loses Thee but he who forsakes Thee." *

And yet we see in this uncontrollable anguish what a deep fountain of love was gushing in his bosom. Could this love only find its proper object, and be purified by the Spirit of God, what a rich ornament and source of blessing must it become to the Church and the world ! At the same time this severe suffering reveals the internal weakness of the Manichæan dogmas and of mere human wisdom. Their consolations cannot reach into the dark hours of trouble ; their promises are convicted

---

* *Confess.* IV. 9 : "*Beatus qui amat Te, et amicum in Te, et inimicum propter Te. Solus enim nullum carum amittit, cui omnes in illo cari sunt, qui non amittitur. Et quis est iste, nisi Deus noster, Deus qui fecit cœlum et terram, et implet ea, quia implendo ea fecit ea ? Te nemo amittit, nisi qui dimittit ; et qui dimittit, quo it, aut quo fugit, nisi a Te placido ad Te iratum ?*"

of falsehood at the brink of the grave. It is true, indeed, that this visitation to his soul passed by without waking him up from his sleep of sin. Still, the death-bed of his friend, which he could not banish from his memory, had certainly the effect of· undermining his faith in the Manichæan system.

CHAPTER VI.

AUGUSTIN LEAVES MANICHÆISM.

In consequence of this loss, which embittered his life in his native city, and impelled also by an ambitious desire for a distinguished career, Augustin went back to Carthage, and opened there a school of forensic eloquence. Amid new relationships and in the society of new friends his wounds were gradually healed, and he went forward in his accustomed path with success, though at times the recklessness of the students gave him great pain.

He appeared also as an author, and published a large philosophical work on *Fitness and Beauty.**

For some time yet he adhered to Manichæism, until at last, in his twenty-ninth year, a crisis arrived. By degrees many doubts had arisen in his mind concerning the system. His confidence in the boasted sanctity of the Manichæan priesthood, the class of the *elect*, was shaken by the rumor of secret vices, which held sway among them, under the hypocritical mask of ·peculiar, ascetic

---

* *De Apto et Pulchro.*

virtues. By the thorough study of philosophy he was able to gain an insight into the many contradictions and untenable points of Manichæan speculation. The notion of evil as a substance co-eternal with God could not satisfy his mind in its struggle after unity.

The Manichæans were unable to solve his doubts, and instead of attempting it, promised to introduce him to their famous bishop, Faustus, who was then regarded as their oracle. He lived at Mileve, a city in the north-western part of Numidia. Augustin himself was very desirous of becoming acquainted with him. This honor was at last granted. They met in Carthage. He discovered in him a brilliant orator and a subtle dialectician, but at the same time a man of moderate culture and without any depth or earnestness of spirit. He compares him to a cup-bearer who, with graceful politeness, presents a costly goblet without anything in it. "With such things," says he, in allusion to his discourses, "my ears are already satiated. They did not appear better because beautifully spoken, nor true because eloquent, nor spiritually wise because the look was expressive and the discourse select. Thou, my God, hast taught me, in wonderful and hidden ways, that a thing should not seem true because portrayed with eloquence, nor false because the breath of the lips is not sounded according to the rules of art; on the other hand, that a thing is not necessarily true because conveyed in rude, nor false because conveyed in brilliant, language; but that wisdom and folly are like wholesome and noxious viands—both may be contained in tasteful or unadorned words, as they in rough or finely-wrought vessels." In the private conversations which he held with Faustus the latter could not answer questions of vital importance to the truth of the Manichæan system, and was obliged to resort to the Socratic confession of ignorance. But that did not agree well with the intellectual arrogance of this sect.

Now, after their boasted champion had so sadly disappointed his expectations, Augustin resolved on breaking with the heresy, although he did not yet formally renounce his place among its adherents.

CHAPTER VII.

ERROR OVERRULED FOR TRUTH.

BEFORE we go on with our church-father let us take a glance at the connection between his wanderings and his later activity in the Church. The marvellous wisdom of God reveals itself in bringing good out of evil and making even the sins and errors of His servants contribute to their own sanctification and an increase of their usefulness. "He overrules the wrath of men for His glory." David's double crime followed by his repentance, Peter's denial wiped out by his bitter tears, Paul's persecuting zeal turned into apostolic devotion, have been an unfailing source of comfort and encouragement to Christians in their struggle with temptation and sin. And yet by no means does this render wickedness excusable. To the question, "Shall we continue in sin that grace may abound?" the Apostle Paul answers with horror, "God forbid!"

The wild, reckless life of Augustin prepared him to look afterward, in the light of grace, far down into the abyss of sin—into the thorough corruption and ingrati-

tude of the human heart.　The bare thought of it must
have deeply troubled him, but the humility that can say
with Paul, "I am the chief of sinners," is one of the
most beautiful pearls in the crown of the Christian character, while spiritual pride and self-righteousness gnaw
like worms at the root of piety.　There is no church-
father who, in regard to deep, unfeigned humility, bears
so much resemblance, or stands so near to the great
apostle of the Gentiles as Augustin.　He manifests in
all his writings a noble renunciation of self in the presence of the Most Holy, and his spirit goes forth in
thankfulness to the superabounding grace which, in spite
of his unworthiness, had drawn him up out of the
depths of corruption and overwhelmed him with mercy.

By his own painful experience he was also fitted to
develop the doctrine of sin, with such rare penetration
and subtlety, to refute the superficial theories of Pelagius,
and thus to render an invaluable service to theology and
the Church.　Further, his theoretical aberration into
Manichæism fitted him to overthrow this false and dangerous system, and to prove, by a striking example, how
fruitless the search after truth must be outside of the
simple, humble faith in Christ.　Thus also was St. Paul,
by his learned Pharisaic education, better qualified than
any other apostle for contending successfully against the
false exegesis and legal righteousness of his Judaistic
opponents.

CHAPTER VIII.

AUGUSTIN A SCEPTIC IN ROME.

AFTER Augustin had lost faith in Manichæism he found himself in the same situation as he was ten years before. There was the same longing after truth, but linked now with a feeling of desolation, a bitter sense of deception, and a large measure of scepticism. He was no longer at ease in Carthage. He hankered after new associations, new scenes, new fountains out of which to drink the good so ardently desired.

This disposition of mind, in connection with a dislike for the rudeness of the Carthaginian students and the exactions of friends, made him resolve on a journey to Rome, where he ventured to hope for a yet more brilliant and profitable career as a rhetorician. Thus he drew nigher to the place where his inward change was to be decided.

He endeavored to conceal his resolution from his mother, who in the mean time had joined him at Carthage. But she found out something about it, and wished either to prevent him from going, or to go with him.

Augustin would listen to neither proposal, and resorted to a trick to carry out his plan. One evening, in the year 383, he went down to the sea-shore, in order to take ship, near the place where two chapels had been dedicated to the memory of the great church-father and martyr, St. Cyprian. His mother suspected his design, and followed him. He pretended that he merely wished to visit a friend on board, and remain with him until his departure. As she was not satisfied with this explana-

tion, and unwilling to turn back alone, he insisted on her
spending at least that one night in the church of the
martyr, and then he would come for her.

While she was there in tears, praying and wrestling
with God to prevent his voyage, Augustin sailed for the
coasts of Italy, and his deceived mother found herself
the next morning alone on the shore of the sea. She
had learned, however, the heavenly art of forgiving, and
believing also, where she could not see. In quiet resignation she returned to the city, and continued to pray for
the salvation of her son, waiting the time when the hand
of Supreme Wisdom would solve the dark riddle.
Though meaning well, she this time erred in her prayer,
for the journey of Augustin was the means of his salvation. The denial of the prayer was, in fact, the answer-
ing of it. Instead of the form, God granted rather the
substance of her petition in the conversion of her son.
" Therefore," says he—" therefore hadst Thou, O God,
regard to the *aim* and *essence* of her desires, and didst
not do what she *then* prayed for, that Thou mightest do
for me what she *continually* implored."

After a prosperous voyage across the Mediterranean
Augustin found lodging in Rome with a Manichæan
host, of the class of the *auditors*, and mingled in the society of the *elect*. He was soon attacked, in the house
of this heretic, by a disease brought on and aggravated
by the agonies of his soul, dissatisfaction with his course
of life, homesickness, and remorse for the heartless
deceit he practised on his mother. The fever rose so
high and signs of approaching dissolution had already
appeared, yet Providence had reserved him for a
long and useful life. " Thou, O God, didst permit me
to recover from that disease, and didst make the son of
Thy handmaid whole, first in body, that he might be-

come one on whom Thou couldst bestow a better and more secure restoration."

Again restored to health, he began to counsel his companions against Manichæism, to which before he had so zealously labored to win over adherents. And yet he could not lead them to the truth. His dislike to the Church had rather increased. The doctrine of the incarnation of the Son of God had become particularly offensive to him, as it was to all Gnostics and Manichæans. He despaired of finding truth in the Church. Yet scepticism could not satisfy him, and so he was tossed wildly between two waters, that would not flow peacefully together. "The more earnestly and perseveringly I reflected on the activity, the acuteness, and the depths of the human soul, the more I was led to believe that truth could not be a thing inaccessible to man, and came thus to the conclusion that the right path to its attainment had not hitherto been discovered, and that this path must be marked out by divine authority. But now the question arose what this divine authority might be, since among so many conflicting sects each professed to teach in its name. A forest full of mazes stood again before my eyes, in which I was to wander about, and to be compelled to tread, which rendered me fearful."

In this unsettled state of mind he felt himself drawn toward the doctrines of the New Academy.* This system, whose representatives were Arcesilaus and Carneades, denied, in most decided opposition to Stoicism, the possibility of an infallible knowledge of any object; it could only arrive at a subjective probability, not truth.

---

* Confess. V. 10 : "Etenim suborta est etiam mihi cogitatio, prudentiores cœteris fuisse illos philosophos, quos Academicos appellant, quod de omnibus dubitandum esse censuerant, nec aliquid veri ab homine comprehendi posse decreverant."

But our church-father could not rest content with a philosophy so sceptical. It only served to give him a deeper sense of his emptiness, and thus, in a negative manner, to pave the way for something better. A change in his external circumstances soon occurred which hastened the great crisis of his life.

After he had been in Rome not quite a year the prefect Symmachus, the eloquent advocate of declining heathenism, was requested to send an able teacher of rhetoric to Milan. The choice fell on Augustin. The recommendation of Manichæan patrons, and still more his trial-speech, obtained for him the honorable and lucrative post. He forsook Rome the more willingly because the manners of the students did not please him. They were accustomed to leave one teacher in the midst of his course, without paying their dues, and go to another.

With this removal to Milan we approach the great crisis in the life of Augustin, when he was freed forever from the fetters of Manichæism and scepticism, and became a glorious light in the Church of Jesus Christ.

CHAPTER IX.

AUGUSTIN IN MILAN—ST. AMBROSE.

In the spring of the year 384 Augustin, accompanied by his old friend Alypius, journeyed to Milan, the second capital of Italy and frequent residence of the Roman Emperor.

The episcopal chair at that place was then filled by one

of the most venerable of the Latin fathers, one who not only earned enduring honors in the sphere of theology, but also in that of sacred poetry and sacred music, and distinguished himself as an ecclesiastical prince by the energetic and wise management of his diocese and his bold defence of the interests of the Church, even against the Emperor himself.

Ambrose was born at Treves, in the year 340, of a very ancient and illustrious family. His father was governor of Gaul, one of the three great dioceses of the Western Roman Empire. When yet a little boy, as he lay sleeping in the cradle with his mouth open, a swarm of bees came buzzing around, and flew in and out of his mouth, without doing him any harm. The father, astonished at the unexpected vanishing of the danger, cried out in a prophetic mood : " Truly, this child, if he lives, will turn out something great !" A similar story is told of Plato. After the early death of the prefect his pious widow moved to Rome with her three children, and gave them a careful education.

Ambrose was marked out for a brilliant worldly career by man, but not by God. After the completion of his studies he made his appearance as an attorney, and acquitted himself so well by his eloquent discourses that Probus, the governor of Italy, appointed him his counsellor. Soon after he conveyed to him the prefecture or viceregency of the provinces of Liguria and Æmilia, in Upper Italy, with the remarkable words, afterward interpreted as an involuntary prophecy : " Go, and act, not as judge, but as bishop." Ambrose administered his office with dignity, justice, and clemency, and won for himself universal esteem.

The Church of Milan was then involved in a battle between Arianism, which denied the divinity of Christ, and Nicene orthodoxy, which maintained the essential equality of the Son with the Father. Augentius, an Arian, had succeeded in driving into exile the Catholic bishop Dionysius, and usurping the episcopal chair. But he died in the year 374.

At the election of a new bishop bloody scenes were apprehended. Ambrose thought it his duty as governor to go into the church and silence the uproar of the parties. His speech to the assembled multitude was suddenly interrupted by the cry of a child—"Ambrose, be bishop!" As swift as lightning the voice of the child became the voice of the people, who with one accord would have him and no other for their chief shepherd.

Ambrose was confounded. He was then still in the class of catechumens, and hence not baptized, and had, moreover, so high an opinion of the dignity and responsibility of the episcopal office that he deemed himself altogether unworthy of it and unfit for it. He resorted to flight, cunning, and the strangest devices to evade the call. But it availed nothing; and when now also the imperial confirmation of the choice arrived, he submitted to the will of God, which addressed him so powerfully through these circumstances. After being baptized by an orthodox bishop, and having run through the different clerical stages, he received episcopal consecration on the eighth day.

His friend Basil, of Cæsarea, was highly rejoiced at the result. "We praise God," so he wrote, "that in all ages He chooses such as are pleasing to Him. He once chose a shepherd and set him up as ruler over His people. Moses, as he tended the goats, was filled with the Spirit of God, and raised to the dignity of a prophet. But in our days He sent out of the royal city, the metropolis of the world, a man of lofty spirit, distinguished by

noble birth and the splendor of riches and by an eloquence, at which the world wonders ; one who renounces
all these earthly glories, and esteems them but loss that he
may win Christ, and accepts, on behalf of the Church,
the helm of a great ship made famous by his faith. So
be of good cheer, O man of God !"

From this time forward until the day of his death,
which occurred on Good Friday of the year 397, Ambrose acted the part of a genuine bishop : he was the
shepherd of the congregation, the defender of the oppressed, the watchman of the Church, the teacher of the
people, the adviser and reprover of kings. He began by
distributing his lands, his gold, and his silver among the
poor. His life was exceedingly severe and simple. He
took no dinner, except on Saturdays, Sundays, and the
festivals of celebrated martyrs. Invitations to banquets
he declined, except when his office required his presence,
and then he set an example of temperance. The day
was devoted to the duties of his calling, the most of the
night to prayer, meditation on divine things, the study
of the Bible and the Greek fathers, and the writing of
theological works. He preached every Sunday, and in
cases of necessity during the week, sometimes twice a
day. To his catechumens he attended with especial care,
but exerted an influence on a wider circle by means of
his writings, in which old Roman vigor, dignity, and
sententiousness were united with a deep and ardent practical Christianity. He was easy of access to all—to the
lowest as well as the highest. His revenues were given
to the needy, whom he called, on this account, his stew-
ards and treasurers. With dauntless heart he battled
against the Arian heresy, and, as the Athanasius of the
West, helped Nicene orthodoxy to its triumph in Upper
Italy.

Such was Ambrose. If any one was fitted for winning over to the Church the highly-gifted stranger who came into his neighborhood, it was he. Augustin visited the bishop, not as a Christian, but as a celebrated and eminent man. He was received by him with paternal kindness, and at once felt himself drawn toward him in love. " Unconsciously was I led to him, my God, by Thee, in order to be consciously led by him to Thee." He also frequently attended his preaching, not that he might be converted by him, and obtain food for his soul, but that he might listen to a beautiful and eloquent sermon. The personal character and renown of Ambrose attracted him. The influence of curiosity was predominant ; and yet it could not but happen that the contents of the discourses also should soon make an impression on him, even against his will.

" I began to love him," says he, " not, indeed, at first as a teacher of the truth, which I despaired of finding in Thy Church, but as a man worthy of my love. I often listened to his public discourses, I confess, not with a pure motive, but only to prove if his eloquence was equal to his fame. I weighed his words carefully, while I had no interest in their meaning, or despised it. I was delighted with the grace of his language, which was more learned, more full of intrinsic value, but in delivery less brilliant and flattering, than that of Faustus, the Manichæan. In regard to the contents, there was no comparison between them ; for while the latter conducted into Manichæan errors, the former taught salvation in the surest way. From sinners, like I was then, salvation is indeed far off ; yet was I gradually and unconsciously drawing near to it. For although it was not my wish to learn *what* he said, but only to hear *how* he said it (this vain interest was left me, who despaired of the truth),

still, along with the words, which I loved, there stole
also into my spirit the substance, which I had no care
for, because I could not separate the two. And while I
opened my heart to receive the eloquence which he uttered, the truth also which he spake found entrance,
though by slow degrees."*

By this preaching the Old Testament was filled with
new light to Augustin. He had imbibed a prejudice
against it from the Manichæans. He regarded it as little
else than a letter that kills. Ambrose unfolded its life-
giving spirit by means of allegorical interpretation, which
was then in vogue among the Fathers, especially those
of the Alexandrian school. Its aim was, above all, to
spiritualize the historical parts of the Bible, and to resolve
the external husk into universal ideas. Thus gross violence was often done to the text, and things were dragged
into the Bible, which, to an unbiassed mind, were not
contained there, at least not in the exact place indicated.
And yet this mode of interpretation was born of the spirit
of faith and reverence, which bowed to the Word of God
as to a source of the most profound truths, and, so far,
was instructive and edifying. To Augustin, who himself
used it freely in his writings, often to capriciousness, although he afterward inclined rather to a cautious, grammatical, and historical apprehension of the Scripture, it
was then very acceptable, and had the good effect of
weaning him still further from Manichæism. He soon
threw it aside altogether. But even the Platonic philosophers, whom he preferred to it, he would not blindly
trust, because "the saving name of Christ was wanting in
them," from which, according to that ineffaceable impression of his pious childhood, he could never separate
the knowledge of the truth.

* *Confess.* V. 13, 14.

CHAPTER X.

AUGUSTIN A CATECHUMEN IN THE CATHOLIC CHURCH.

WE would suppose that he was now ready to cast himself into the arms of the Church, which approached him
by a representative so worthy and so highly gifted. But
he had not yet come so far. Various difficulties stood in
the way. To think of God as a purely spiritual substance gave him peculiar trouble. In this he was yet
under the influence of Manichæism, which clothed the
spiritual idea of God in the garb of sense.

Nevertheless, he took a considerable step in advance.
He enrolled himself in the class of the catechumens, to
which he had already belonged when a boy, and resolved
to remain there until he could arrive at a decision in his
own soul.* He says of his condition at this time, that
he had come so far already that any capable teacher
would have found in him a most devoted and teachable
scholar.

Thus did Augustin resign himself to the maternal care
of the communion in which he had received his early,
never-forgotten religious impressions. It could not happen otherwise than, after an honest search, he should at
last discover in her the supernatural glory, which, to the
offence of the carnal understanding, was concealed under
the form of a servant. A man possessed of his ardent
longing after God, his tormenting thirst for truth and
peace of mind, could obtain rest only in the asylum

---

* *Confess.* V. 14 : " *Statui ergo tamdiu esse catechumenus in catholica
ecclesia, mihi a parentibus commendata, donec aliquid certi eluceret, quo
cursum dirigerem.*"

founded by God Himself, and see there all his desires
fulfilled beyond his highest hopes.

The Church had then emerged from the bloody field
of those witnesses who had joyfully offered up their lives
to show their gratitude and fidelity to the Lord who had
died for them. Their heroic courage, which overcame
the world; their love, which was stronger than death;
their patience, which endured cruel tortures without a
murmur, as lambs led to the slaughter; and their hope,
which burst out in songs of triumph at the stake and on
the cross, were yet fresh in her memory. Everywhere
altars and chapels were erected to perpetuate their virtues. From a feeling of thankfulness for the victory, so
dearly purchased by their death, and in the consciousness
of an uninterrupted communion with the glorified warriors, their heavenly birthdays were celebrated.* While
heathenism, in the pride of its power, its literature, and
its art, was falling into decay, the youthful Church, sure
of her promise of eternal duration, pressed triumphantly
forward into a new era, to take possession of the wild
hordes of the invading nations who destroyed the Roman
Empire, and communicate to them, along with faith in
the Redeemer, civilization, morality, and the higher
blessings of life. The most noble and profound spirits
sought refuge in her communion, in which alone they
could find rest for their souls and quench their thirst
after truth. She fearlessly withstood the princes and
potentates of earth, and reminded them of righteousness
and judgment. In that stormy and despotic period she
afforded shelter to the oppressed, was a kind and loving
mother to the poor, the widow, and the orphan, and
opened her treasures to all who needed help. They who

---

* So were the days of their death called.

were weary of life found in the peaceful cells of her monasteries, in communion with pilgrims of like spirit, an undisturbed retreat, where they could give themselves wholly up to meditation on divine things. Thus she cared for all classes, and brought consolation and comfort into every sphere of life. She zealously persevered in preaching and exhorting, in the education of youth for a better world, in prayer and in intercession for the bitterest enemies, and in ascriptions of glory to the Holy Trinity.

Her devotion concentrated itself on the festivals, recurring yearly in honor of the great facts of the Gospel, especially on Easter and Whitsuntide, when multitudes of catechumens, of both sexes and all ages, clad in white garments, the symbol of purity, were received into the ranks of Christ's warriors, amid fervent prayers and animating hymns of praise. The prince bowed with the peasant in baptism before the common Lord ; the famous scholar sat like a child among the catechumens ; and blooming virgins, "those lilies of Christ," as Ambrose calls them, made their vow before the altar to renounce the world and live for the heavenly bridegroom. The activity of Ambrose was in this respect attended by the richest results. He would frequently, on the solemn night before Easter, have as many incorporated into the communion of the Church by baptism as five other bishops together.

The Church of that time was still an undivided unity, without excluding, however, great diversity of gifts and powers. And this enabled her to overcome so victoriously heresies, schisms, persecutions, and the collected might of heathenism itself. One body and one spirit, one Lord, one faith, one baptism, one God and Father of all—this declaration of the apostle was more applicable to the first centuries of the Church than to later periods. The dweller on the Rhine found on the borders of the African desert, and the Syrian on the shores of the Rhone, the same confession of faith, the same sanctifying power, and the same ritual of worship. The Christian of the fourth century felt himself in living communion with all the mighty dead, who had long before departed in the service of the same Lord. That age had no idea of an interruption in the history of God's kingdom, a sinking away of the life-stream of Christ. From the heart of God and His Son it has rolled down, from the days of the apostles, through the veins of the Church Catholic, amid certain infallible signs, in one unbroken current to the present, in order gradually to fertilize the whole round of earth, and empty itself into the ocean of eternity.

And yet we have just as little reason to think the Church at that time free from faults and imperfections as at any other period. Some dream, indeed, of a golden age of spotless purity. But such an age has never been, and will only first appear after the general resurrection. Even the Apostolic Church was, in regard to its membership, by no means absolutely pure and holy ; for we need only read attentively and with unbiassed mind any Epistle of the New Testament or the letters to the seven churches in the Apocalypse, in order to be convinced that they collectively reproved the congregations to which they were sent, for various faults, excrescences, and perversions, and warned them of manifold errors, dangers, and temptations. When, moreover, through the conversion of Constantine, the great mass of the heathen world crowded into the Church, they dragged along with them also a vast amount of corruption. A very sad and dreary picture

of the Christianity of the Nicene period can be drawn
from the writings of the fathers of the fourth century
(Gregory Nazianzen, for example), so that the modern
Church in comparison appears in many respects like a
great improvement.   The march of Christianity is
steadily onward.

In spite of all these defects there were yet remedies
and salt enough to preserve the body from decay.   The
militant Church, in her continuous conflict with a sinful
world, must ever authenticate and develop the power of
genuine sanctity, and this she did during the Nicene
period.   We cannot mistake the agency of the Holy
Spirit, who, amid the stormy and passionate battles with
Arianism and semi-Arianism, at last helped the Nicene
faith to victory.   And we cannot refuse genuine admiration to those great heroes of the fourth century, an
Athanasius, a Basil, a Gregory of Nyssa, a Gregory of
Nazianzum, a Chrysostom, an Ambrose, a Jerome, who
were distinguished as much by earnestness and dignity of
character and depth and vigor of piety as by their eminent learning and culture, and who are, even to this day,
gratefully honored by the Greek, the Roman, and the
Protestant communions as true church-*fathers*.   Notwithstanding all the corruption in her bosom, the Catholic Church of that age was still immeasurably elevated
above heathenism, sinking into hopeless ruin, and the
conceited and arrogant schools of the Gnostics and Manichæans ; for she, and she alone, was the bearer of the
divine-human life-powers of the Christian religion, and
the hope of the world.

CHAPTER XI.

ARRIVAL OF MONNICA.

Such was the state of the Church when Augustin entered the class of catechumens and listened attentively to her doctrines. His good genius, Monnica, soon came to Milan, as one sent by God. She could no longer stay in Africa without her son, and embarked for Italy. While at sea a storm arose, which made the oldest sailors tremble. But she, feeling strong and secure under the protection of the Almighty, encouraged them all, and confidently predicted a happy termination to the voyage ; for God had promised it to her in a vision. In Milan she found her son delivered from the snares of Manichæism, but not yet a believing professor. She was highly rejoiced, and accepted the partial answer of her tearful prayers as a pledge of their speedy and complete fulfilment. " My son," said she, with strong assurance, " I believe in Christ, that before I depart this life I shall see thee become a believing, Catholic Christian." *

She found favor with Ambrose, who often spoke of her with great respect, and thought the son happy who had such a mother. She regularly attended his ministrations, and willingly gave up certain usages, which, though observed by her at home, were not in vogue at Milan, such as fasting on Saturdays and love-feasts at the graves of the martyrs. With renewed fervor and confi-

---

* *Confess.* VI. 1: " *Placidissime et pectore pleno fiduciæ respondit mihi, credere se in Christo, quod priusquam de hac vita emigraret me visura esset fidelem catholicum.*"

dence she now prayed to God, who had already led the
darling of her heart to the gates of the sanctuary. She
was soon to witness the fulfilment of her desires.

———

CHAPTER XII.

MORAL CONFLICTS—PROJECT OF MARRIAGE.

AUGUSTIN continued to listen to the discourses of Ambrose and visit him at his house, although the bishop,
on account of pressing duties, could not enter so fully
as he wished into his questions and doubts. He now
obtained a more just idea of the doctrines of the Scriptures and the Church than the perversions of the Manichæans had afforded him. He saw " that all the knots
of cunning misrepresentation which these modern be-
trayers of the Divine Word had tied up could be un-
loosed, and that for so many years he had been assailing,
not the real faith of the Church, but chimeras of a fleshly
imagination." He now first began to prize and comprehend the Bible in some measure, while before it had
been to him a disagreeable volume, sealed with seven
seals ; and such it ever is to all those who wilfully tear
it loose from living Christianity, and drag it into the
forum of the carnal understanding, " which perceives
not the things of the Spirit of God," and thus factiously
constitute themselves judges over it, instead of surrender-
ing themselves to it in humble obedience.

Meanwhile he had many practical and theoretical struggles to pass through before reaching a final decision.
About this time, in conjunction with his friends, among

whom were Alypius, who had come with him to Milan, and Nebridius, who had lately left Africa, in order to live together with Augustin, " in the most ardent study of truth and wisdom," he resolved to form a philosophical union, and, in undisturbed retirement, with a community of goods, to devote himself exclusively to the pursuit of truth. In such a self-created ideal world, which commended itself to the lofty imagination of one so gifted and noble as Augustin was, he sought a substitute for the reality of Christianity and the deeper earnestness of practical life and activity. " Diverse thoughts were thus in our hearts, but Thy counsel, O God, abides in eternity. According to that counsel Thou didst laugh at ours, and work out Thine own, to bestow on us the Spirit at the set time." " While the winds were blowing from every quarter and tossing my heart to and fro, time went by, and I delayed in turning to the Lord, and put off living in Thee from day to day, and did not put off dying daily in myself. Desiring a life of blessedness, I shunned the place where it dwelt, and sought it by flying from it." *

The romantic scheme fell to pieces, because the friends could not agree as to whether marriage ought to be wholly forbidden in their philosophical hermitage, as Alypius desired, in the fashion of the ascetic piety of that age, or not, as Augustin proposed. He was unable then to give up the love of women. " I believed I would become very unhappy if I was deprived of the embraces of woman, and I did not consider the medicine of Thy grace for the healing of this weakness, for I was inexperienced ; for I esteemed continency an affair of natural ability of which I was not conscious, and was foolishly

---

* *Confess.* VI. 11 : " *Amando beatam vitam, timebam illam in sede sua, et ab ea fugiens quærebam cam.*"

ignorant of what the Scripture says (Wisdom viii. 21),
that no one can be continent unless God gives him power.
Surely, Thou wouldst have given it to me had I prayed
to Thee with inward groaning, and with firm faith cast
my care upon Thee !" *

On this account Augustin resolved to enter into formal
wedlock, though for certain reasons the resolution was
never carried into effect.

His mother, who, in common with the whole Church
of that era, regarded perfect abstinence as a higher
grade of virtue, still, under the circumstances, eagerly
laid hold of the plan. In the haven of marriage she
believed him secure from debauchery, and then every
hindrance to his baptism, which she so ardently desired,
was also taken away.

Both looked around for a suitable match. The choice
was not easily made, for Augustin wished to find beauty,
amiability, refinement, and some wealth united in one
person. In this matter the mother, as usual, took counsel of God in prayer. At last a lady was discovered an-
swerable to their wishes, who also gave her consent, but
because of her youth the nuptials had to be postponed
for two years longer.

Augustin immediately discharged his mistress, whom
he had brought with him from Carthage, and who, as
one would think, was best entitled to the offer of his
hand. This conduct is a serious blot on his character,
according to our modern notions of morality. But neither
he nor Monnica looked upon it in that light, and were
unconscious of doing any wrong. The unhappy outcast,
who appears to have loved him truly, and had been faithful to him, as he to her, during the thirteen years of

---

* *Confess.* VI. 11.

their intercourse, returned to Africa with a heavy heart, and vowed that she would never know any other man. Their natural son, Adeodatus, she left with his father.

Just after the separation Augustin felt with bleeding heart the strength of his unlawful attachment. So strong had the power of sensuality become in him through habit, that neither the recollections of the departed nor respect for his bride could restrain him from forming a new immoral connection for the interval. Along with this carnal lust came also the seductions of ambition and a longing after a brilliant career in the world. He felt very miserable; he must have been ashamed before his own better self, before God and man. "But the more miserable I felt, the nearer didst Thou come to me, O God." The Disposer of his life had His hand over all this. "I thought, and Thou wert with me; I sighed, and Thou heardst me; I was tossed about, yet Thou didst pilot me; I wandered on the broad way, and still Thou didst not reject me."

CHAPTER XIII.

MENTAL CONFLICTS.

YET more violent and painful were his theoretical conflicts, the tormenting doubts of his philosophic spirit.

The question concerning the origin of evil, which once attracted him to the Manichæans, was again brooded over with renewed interest. The heresy that evil is a substance, and co-eternal with God, he had rejected. But whence then was it? The Church found its origin in the will of the creature, who was in the beginning good, and of his own free choice estranged himself from God. But here the question arose, Is not the possibility of evil, imprinted by God in its creation on the will, itself already the germ of evil? Or could not God, as the Almighty, have so created the will as to render the fall impossible? How can He then be a Being of perfect goodness? And if we transfer the origin of evil, as the Church does, from the human race to Satan, through whose temptation Adam fell, the difficulty is not thereby settled, but only pushed further back. Whence, then, the Devil? and if he was first transformed from a good angel into a devil by a wicked will, whence then that wicked will?

Here he was again met by the spectre of Gnostic and Manichæan dualism, but soon reverted to the idea of the absolute God, whom he had made the immovable ground-pillar of his thinking, and who naturally cannot suffer the admission of a second absolute existence. Perhaps evil is a mere shadow. But how can anything unreal and empty prepare such fears and torments for the conscience?

He revolved such questions in his mind, and found no peace. "Thou, my God—Thou alone knowest what I suffered, but no one among men." He was not able to communicate fully the tumult of his soul even to his most intimate friends. But these conflicts had the good effect of driving him to prayer and strengthening in him the conviction that mind, left to itself, can never reach a satisfactory result.

CHAPTER XIV.

INFLUENCE OF PLATONISM.

About this time, somewhere in the beginning of the year 386, he fell in with certain Platonic and New Platonic writings, translated into Latin by the rhetorician Victorinus, who afterward was converted to Christianity. No doubt he had a general acquaintance with this philosophy before. But now, for the first time, he studied it earnestly in its original sources, to which he was introduced by an admiring disciple. He himself says that it kindled in him an incredible ardor.[*]

Platonism is beyond dispute the noblest product of heathen speculation, and stands in closer contact with Revelation than any other philosophical system of antiquity. It is in some measure an unconscious prophecy of Christ, in whom alone its sublime ideals can ever become truth and reality. The Platonic philosophy is distinguished by a lofty ideality, which raises man above the materialistic doings and sensual views of every-day life into the invisible world, to the contemplation of truth, beauty, and virtue. It is genuine *philosophy*, or love of wisdom, home-sickness—deep longing and earnest search after truth. It reminds man of his original likeness to God, and thus gives him a glimpse of the true end of all his endeavor.

Platonism also approaches Revelation in several of its

---

[*] *Contr. Academ.* II. 5 : " *E'iam mihi ipsi de me ipso incredibile incendium in me concitarunt.*" Comp. my *History of the Apost. Church,* p. 150 sqq., and my *Church History,* vol. II. p. 95 sqq., where the relation of Platonism to Christianity and to the Church Fathers is discussed in detail.

doctrines, at least in the form of obscure intimation. We may here mention its presentiment of the unity, and, in a certain measure, the trinity of the Divine Being; the conception that the world of ideas is alone true and eternal, and the world of sense its copy ; and further, that the human soul has fallen away from a condition of original purity, and merited its present suffering existence in the prison of the body ; but that it should have long-ing aspirations after its home, the higher world, free itself from the bonds of sense, and strive after the high-est spiritual and eternal good.

Hence it was no wonder that Platonism to many culti-vated heathens and some of the most prominent fathers, especially in the Greek Church, became a theoretical schoolmaster for leading to Christ, as the Law was a practical schoolmaster to the Jews. It delivered Au-gustin completely from the bondage of Manichæan dual-ism and Academic scepticism, and turned his gaze inward and upward. In the height of his enthusiasm he be-lieved that he had already discovered the hidden foun-tain of wisdom. But he had soon to learn that not the abstract knowledge of the truth, but living in it, could alone give peace to the soul ; and that this end could only be reached in the way of divine revelation and practical experience of the heart.

Although the Platonic philosophy contained so many elements allied to Christianity, there were yet two im-portant points not found therein : first, the great mys-tery, the Word made flesh ; and then love, resting on the basis of humility.* The Platonic philosophy held up before him beautiful ideals, without giving him power

* *Confess.* VII. 20 : " *Ubi enim erat illa caritas ædificans a funda-mento humilitatis, quod est Christus Jesus ? Aut quando illi libri [Pla-tonici] docerent me eam ?*"

to attain them.   If he attempted to seize them ungodly
impulses would suddenly drag him down again into the
mire.

CHAPTER XV.

STUDY OF THE SCRIPTURES.

Thus the admonition to study the Holy Scriptures was
addressed to him once more, and in a stronger tone than
ever.   He now gave earnest heed to it, and drew near
the holy volume with deep reverence and a sincere desire for salvation.*

He was principally carried away with the study of the
Epistles of St. Paul, and read them through collectively
with the greatest care and admiration.   Here he found
all those truths which addressed him in Platonism no
longer obscurely foreshadowed, but fulfilled ; and yet
much more besides.   Here he found Christ as the Medi-
ator between God and man, between heaven and earth,
who alone can give us power to attain those lofty ideals
and embody them in life.   Here he read that masterly de-
lineation of the conflict between the spirit and the flesh
(Rom. vii.), which was literally confirmed by his own experience.   Here he learned to know aright the depth of
the ruin and the utter impossibility of being delivered
from it by any natural wisdom or natural strength, and,
at the same time, the great remedy which God graciously
offers to us in His beloved Son.

Such light, such consolation, and such power the Pla-

---

* *Confess.* VII. 21: "*Itaque avidissime arripui venerabilem stilum
Spiritus tui, et præ cæteris Apostolum Paulum,*" etc.

tonic writings had never yielded. "On their pages," he says very beautifully, in the close of the seventh book of his *Confessions*, "no traces of piety like this can be discovered ; tears of penitence ; Thy sacrifice, the broken spirit ; the humble and the contrite heart ; the healing of the nations ; the Bride, the City of God ; the earnest of the Holy Spirit ; the cup of our salvation. No one sings there : 'Truly my soul waiteth upon God ; from Him cometh my salvation ; He only is my rock and my salvation ; He is my high tower ; I shall not be greatly moved.' (Ps. lxii. 1, 2.) There no one hears the invitation : 'Come unto me, all ye that labor and are heavy-laden, and I will give you rest.' (Matt. xi. 28.) They [the Platonists] disdain to learn of Him who is meek and lowly in heart ; they cannot imagine why the lowly should teach the lowly, nor understand what is meant by His taking the form of a servant. For Thou hast hidden it from the wise and prudent, and revealed it unto babes. It is one thing to see afar off, from the summit of a woody mountain, the fatherland of peace, and without any path leading thither, to wander around lost and weary among byways, haunted by lions and dragons, that lurk in ambush for their prey ; and quite another to keep safely on a road that leads thither, guarded by the care of a Celestial Captain, where no robbers, who have forsaken the heavenly army, ever lie in wait. This made a wonderful impression on my spirit, when I read the humblest of Thine Apostles (1 Cor. xv. 9), and considered Thy works, and saw the depths of sin."

CHAPTER XVI.

AUGUSTIN'S CONVERSION.

WE now stand on the threshold of his conversion. Theoretically he was convinced of the truth of the doctrines of the Church, but practically had yet to undergo, in his bitter experience, the judgment of St. Paul: "The flesh lusteth against the spirit, and the spirit against the flesh." (Gal. v. 17.) No sooner did his soul rise into the pure ether of communion with God than the cords of sense drew him down again into the foul atmosphere of earth. "The world," said he, "lost its charms before Thy sweetness and before the glory of Thy house, which I had learned to love; but I was yet bound by strong ties to a woman." "I had found the beautiful pearl; I should have sold all I possessed to buy it, and yet I hesitated."

Amid the tumult of the world he often sighed after solitude. Desiring counsel, and unwilling to disturb the indefatigable Ambrose, he betook himself to the venerable priest Simplicianus, who had grown gray in the service of his Master. The priest described to him, for his encouragement, the conversion of his friend Victorinus, a learned teacher of rhetoric at Rome, and translator of the Platonic writings, who had passed over from the Platonic philosophy to a zealous study of the Scriptures, and cordially embraced the Saviour with a sacrifice of great worldly gain. For a long time he believed he could be a Christian without joining the Church, and when Simplicianus replied to him: "I will not count you a Christian before I see you in the Church of Christ," Victorinus asked with a smile: "Do the walls,

then, make Christians?" * But afterward he came to
see that he who does not confess Christ openly before the
world need not hope to be confessed by Him before His
Heavenly Father (Matt. x. 32, 33), and therefore submitted in humble faith to the washing of baptism.

Augustin wished to do likewise, but his will was not
yet strong enough. He compares his condition to that
of a man drunk with sleep, who wishes to rise up, but
now for the first time rightly feels the sweetness of slumber, and sinks back again into its arms. In a still more
warning and pressing tone the voice sounded in his ears :
" Awake, thou that sleepest, and arise from the dead,
and Christ shall shine upon thee" (Eph. v. 14) ; but he
answered lazily : " Soon, yes, soon ! only wait a little ;"
and the *soon* passed on into hours, days, and weeks. In
vain his inward man delighted in the law of God, for
another law in his members warred against the law of his
mind, and brought him into captivity to the law of sin.
(Rom. vii. 22, 23.) His disquietude rose higher and
higher ; his longing became violent agony. Oftentimes
he would tear his hair, smite his forehead, wring his
hands about his knees, and cry out despairingly : " O
wretched man that I am ! who shall deliver me out of
the body of this death ?" (Rom. vii. 24.)

These conflicts, in connection with the weight of his
literary labors, had exerted such an injurious influence on
his health that he began to think seriously of resigning
his post as a rhetorician.

One day, as he sat in a downcast mood with his bosom
friend Alypius, who was involved in similar struggles,

---

* *Confess.* VIII. 2 : " *Ergo parietes faciunt Christianos ?*" This passage is sometimes torn from its connection and misused for a purpose
directly opposite ; since Augustin quotes it to show that a man
could not be a Christian without joining the visible Church.

their countryman Pontitianus, a superior officer in the
Roman army, and at the same time a zealous Christian,
entered the chamber. He was surprised, instead of a
classic author or a Manichæan writer, to see the Epistles
of Paul lying on the table. He began a religious conversation, and in the course of his remarks took occasion
to speak of the Egyptian hermit Anthony (died 356),
who, in literal pursuance of the Saviour's advice to the
rich young man (Matt. xix. 21), had given up all his
property in order to live to the Lord unrestricted and
undisturbed, in solitude, and there to work out the salvation of his soul. The two friends had as yet heard nothing of the wonderful saint of the desert, the venerable
father of monachism, and just as little of a cloister outside of the walls of Milan, under the supervision of Ambrose, and were now charmed and ashamed at the information. Their countryman related further how, during
his stay at Treves, two of his friends, who were both
engaged to be married, obtained, on a visit to a cell, the
biography of Anthony ascribed to Athanasius, the great
"father of orthodoxy," and on reading it fell so in love
with the contemplative life and the higher perfection
there portrayed, that they threw up their commissions in
the army and took leave of the world forever. Their
brides did likewise.

This was a sting for the conscience of Augustin. The
soldiers and their brides had heard the call of the Lord
only once, and obeyed it immediately. And he? It
was now more than twelve years since the *Hortensius* of
Cicero had stirred him up so powerfully to search after
truth, and ever clearer and clearer the voice of the Good
Shepherd had sounded in his ears. And yet his will rose
up in rebellion ; he was not ready to renounce the world
wholly, but desired to retain at least some of its pleasures.

Pontitianus left the house. Then the storm in the soul of Augustin broke loose with greater violence, and expressed itself in the features of his countenance, his looks, and his gestures still more than in his words. " What has happened to us ?" said he to Alypius—" what is it ? What hast thou heard ? The unlearned rise up and lay hold of the kingdom of heaven, and we, with our heartless knowledge—see how we wallow in flesh and blood ! Shall we be ashamed to follow them because they have gone before, and not ashamed not to follow them at all ?" *

After he had said this, and more in a similar strain, he rushed out with the Epistles of Paul in his hand into an adjoining garden, where no one would be likely to interrupt the agitation of his soul until God Himself should allay it. For it was, as he said, despair or salvation, death or life. Alypius followed in his footsteps.

" We removed as far as possible from the house. I groaned in spirit, full of stormy indignation that I had not entered into covenant and union with Thee, my God, and all my bones cried out ; thither must thou go ! But it was not possible to go by ship, or wagon, or on foot, as we go to any place we please. For going thither and coming there is nothing else than to *will* to go thither, and to will with *full* power—not to waver and be tossed to and fro with a divided will, which now rises up and now sinks down in the struggle." † He was angry at the perverseness of his will : " The spirit orders the body, and it obeys instantly ; the spirit orders itself, and

---

* *Confess.* VIII. 8.

† *Confess.* VIII. 8 : " *Nam non solum ire, verum etiam pervenire illuc, nihil erat aliud, quam velle ire, sed velle fortiter et integre ; non semisaucium hac atque hac versare et jactare voluntatem, parte adsurgente cum alia parte cadente luctantem.*"

it refuses. The spirit orders the hand to move, and it does it so quickly that one can scarcely distinguish between the act and the command ; the spirit commands the spirit to will, and although the same, it will not do it. Whence this monstrosity ? It is a disease of the spirit that prevents it from rising up ; the will is split and divided ; thus there are two wills in conflict with each other, one good and one evil, and I myself it was who willed and who did not will.''

Thus was he pulled hither and thither, accusing himself more severely than ever, and turning and rolling in his fetters until they should be wholly broken, by which, indeed, he was no longer *wholly* bound, but only *yet*.

And when he had thus dragged up all his misery from its mysterious depths, and gathered it before the eye of his soul, a huge storm arose that discharged itself in a flood of tears.*

In such a frame of mind he wished to be alone with his God, and withdrew from Alypius into a retired corner of the garden. Here Augustin, he knew not how, threw himself down upon the earth, under a fig-tree, and gave free vent to his tears. "Thou, my Lord," he cried, with sobbing voice, "how long yet ? O Lord, how long yet wilt Thou be angry ? Remember not the sins of my youth ! How long ? how long ? To-morrow, and again, to-morrow ? Why not to-day, why not now ? Why not in this hour put an end to my shame ?" †

---

* *Confess.* VIII. 12 : " *Oborta est procella ingens, ferens ingentem imbrem lacrymarum.*"

† *Confess.* VIII. 12 : " *Et non quidem his verbis, sed in hac sententia multa dixi tibi :' Et tu Domine, usquequo ? Usquequo, Domine, irasceris in finem ? Ne memor fueris iniquitatum nostrarum antiquarum ! Sentiebam enim eis me teneri. Jactabam voces miserabiles : Quamdiu ? Quamdiu ? Cras et cras ? Quare non modo ? Quare non hac hora finis turpitudinis meae ? Dicebam hæc, et fiebam amarissima contritione cordis mei.*"

Thus he prayed, supplicated, sighed, wrestled, and wept bitterly. They were the birth-pangs of the new life. From afar he saw the Church in the beauty of holiness. The glorified spirits of the redeemed, who had been snatched from the abyss by the All-merciful and transplanted into a heavenly state of being, beckoned to him. Still more powerfully the longing burned within him; still more hot and rapidly beat the pulse of desire after the Saviour's embrace; as a weary, hunted stag after the fresh water-brooks, so panted his heart after the living God and a draught from the chalice of His grace.

The hour of deliverance had now come. The Lord had already stretched out His hand to tear asunder the last cords that bound his prodigal son to the world, and press him to a warm, true father's heart.

As Augustin was thus lying in the dust and ashes of repentance, and agonizing with his God in prayer, he suddenly heard from a neighboring house, as though from some celestial height, the sweet voice, whether of a boy or a maiden he knew not, calling out again and again, "*Tolle lege, tolle lege!*" *i.e.,* "Take and read." It was a voice from God that decided his heart and life. "Then I repressed," so he further relates in the last chapter of the eighth book of his *Confessions,* "the gush of tears, and raised myself up, while I received the word as nothing else than a divine injunction to open the Scriptures and read the first chapter that would catch my eye. I had heard how Anthony, once accidentally present during the reading of the gospel in church, had felt himself admonished, as though what was read had been specially aimed at him: 'Go, sell that thou hast, and give to the poor, and thou shalt have treasure in heaven; and come, follow me' (Matt. xix. 20), and that, by this oracle, he had been immediately converted, my God, to Thee.''

He hastened to the place where he had left the Holy Book, and where Alypius sat ; snatched it up, opened, and read : "LET US WALK HONESTLY, AS IN THE DAY ; NOT IN REVELLING AND DRUNKENNESS, NOT IN CHAMBERING AND WANTONNESS, NOT IN STRIFE AND JEALOUSY. BUT PUT YE ON THE LORD JESUS CHRIST, AND MAKE NOT PROVISION FOR THE FLESH, TO FULFIL THE LUSTS THEREOF.'' (Rom. xiii. 13, 14.)*

This passage of the Epistle to the Romans was exactly suited to his circumstances. It called on him to renounce his old, wild life, and begin a new life with Christ. He found still more in it, according to the ascetic spirit of the age, and resolved to renounce all the honors and pleasures of the world, even his contemplated marriage, in order to devote himself, without restraint, to the service of the Lord and His Church, and, if possible, to attain the highest grade of moral perfection.†

He read no further. That single word of God was

---

* After the original and the Vulgate : " *et carnis providentiam ne feceritis in concupiscentiis*," which Augustin, in his present condition, understood as a challenge to renounce completely every desire of the flesh. Luther, on the contrary, has translated it : " *Wartet des Leibes, doch also, dass er nicht geil werde*," which gives a different sense. But in such a case σῶμα would be used in the Greek instead of σάρξ, and the conjunctive particle μή would stand after and not before πρόνοιαν.

† *Confess.* VIII. 12: "*Convertisti me ad te, ut nec uxorem quaererem, nec aliquam spem sœculi hujus*," etc. Anthony, whose example had wrought powerfully in the conversion of Augustin, had, likewise, in literal accordance with the words of Christ (Matt. xix. 21), sold all that he had, and given it to the poor. According to the views of the ancient Church, which can be traced back as far as the second century, voluntary poverty, celibacy, and martyrdom were the way to a more literal following of Christ and a higher grade of holiness and bliss.

sufficient to decide his whole future. The gloomy clouds of doubt and despondency rolled away ; the forgiveness of his sins was sealed to him ; peace and joy streamed into his bosom. With his finger on the passage read, he shut the book, and told Alypius what had happened. The latter wished to read the words, and hit upon the next following verse (xiv. 1), " Him that is weak in the faith receive ye." He applied the warning to himself.

Both hastened, in the first ardor of conversion, to Monnica. The faithful soul must hear the glad tidings before others. She cried aloud and exulted, and her heart overflowed with thankfulness to the Lord, who, at last, after long, long delay, had answered beyond her prayers and comprehension.

This occurred in September of the year 386, in the thirty-third year of his life. Truly says Augustin : " All who worship Thee must, when they hear this, cry out : Blessed be the Lord, in heaven and on earth ; great and wonderful is His name !"

CHAPTER XVII.

SOJOURN IN THE COUNTRY.

Augustin continued in office the few remaining weeks, till the autumnal holidays, and then handed in his resignation as public teacher of forensic eloquence, partly on account of a weakness of the breast, but chiefly because he had firmly resolved to consecrate himself henceforth wholly and entirely to the pursuit of divine things.

Along with his mother, his son, and his brother Navigius, Alypius, and other friends, he now withdrew to Cassiciacum, a villa lying near Milan, which belonged to his friend Verecundus.* He passed six months there under the serene Italian sky, in view of the glorious Swiss Alps, devoted to quiet meditation and preparation for the rite of holy baptism.

He had asked the advice of Ambrose as to what parts of Scripture he ought to study under his peculiar circumstances. The bishop recommended the Prophecies of Isaiah. But as Augustin could not rightly understand them he selected the Psalms, and found there just what he desired—the hallowed expression of his deepest religious feelings, from the low, sad wail of penitence and contrition up to the inspiring song of praise to the Divine Mercy. Half the night he spent in their study and in pious meditation, and enjoyed most blessed hours of intimate communion with God. He now mourned over and pitied the Manichæans for being so blind in regard to the Old Testament, which they rejected. "I wished only," he once thought, "they could have been in my neighborhood without my knowing it, and could have seen my face and heard my voice when in that retirement I read the Fourth Psalm, and how that Psalm wrought upon me."

A great part of the day he devoted to the education of two young men from his native city. His propensity for speculative meditation was so strong that he resorted with his company, in good weather, to the shade of a large tree, and in bad to the halls of the baths belonging to the villa, and, walking up and down in the freest

---

* Probably near the town Casciago in Lombardy, at the foot of a group of hills, from which there is a sublime view of the Monte Rosa.

manner, delivered discourses on those philosophical subjects which stood in the nearest relation to the most weighty practical interests of the heart—such as the knowledge of the truth, the idea of genuine wisdom, the life of blessedness and the way to it. Monnica took part in the discussion, and showed a rare degree of good sense and strength of intellect, so that the men forgot her sex and thought that "some great man was in their circle." These discourses were written down, and thus the earliest works of the great theologian, mostly philosophical in their contents, took their rise.

Of these the most important are : First, three books against the sceptical school of the Later Academy (*Contra Academicos*), which denied the possibility of knowing the truth. In opposition it was shown that scepticism either abrogates itself or, in a modified form, as a scheme of probabilities, bears witness to the existence of truth, for the probable must presuppose the true. Not the mere striving after truth, only the possession of it, can render happy. But it is only to be found in God, since He alone is happy who is in God and God in Him. The second discourse is a tract on the Life of Blessedness (*De Beata Vita*), in which these latter thoughts are further developed. And last, his " Soliloquies," or Discourses with his own Soul, concerning God, concerning the highest good, concerning his own nature, immortality, and the like. From these we will quote a single passage, to show the state of his mind at that time.

" O God, Creator of the world"—thus he prayed to the Lord— " grant me, first of all, grace to call upon Thee in a manner well-pleasing unto Thee ; that I may so conduct myself, that Thou mayest hear and then help me. Thou God, through whom all, that cannot be of itself, rises into being ; who even dost not suffer to fall into destruction what would destroy itself ; who never workest evil and rulest over the power of evil ; who revealest unto the few who seek after a true existence that evil can be overcome ; God, to whom the universe, in spite of evil, is perfect ; God, whom what can love, loves consciously or unconsciously ; God, in whom all is, and whom yet neither the infamy of the creature can disgrace, nor his wickedness defile, nor his error lead astray ; God, who hast preserved the knowledge of the truth for the pure alone ; Father of truth, Father of wisdom, Father of true and perfect life, Father of blessedness, Father of the good and the beautiful, Father of our awakening and enlightening, Father of the promise by which we are encouraged to return unto Thee, I invoke Thee, O Truth, in which and from which and by which all is true, that is true ; O Wisdom, in which and from which and by which all is wise, that is wise ; O true and most perfect Life, in which and from which and by which all lives, that lives ; O Blessedness, in which and from which and by which all is blessed, that is blessed ; O Beauty and Goodness, in which and from which and by which all is good and beautiful, that is good and beautiful ; O spiritual Light, in which and from which and by which all is spiritually light, that is spiritually light ; God, from whom to turn away is to fall, to whom to turn again is to rise, in whom to remain is to endure ; God, from whom to withdraw is to die, to whom to return is to live again, in whom to dwell is to live ; O God, Thou who dost sanctify and prepare us for an everlasting inheritance, bow down Thyself to me in pity ! Come to my help, Thou one, eternal, true Essence, in whom there is no discord, no confusion, no change, no need, no death, but the highest unity, the highest purity, the highest durability, the highest fulness, the highest life. · Hear, hear, hear me, my God, my Lord, my King, my Father, my Hope, my Desire, my Glory, my Habitation, my Home, my Salvation, my Light, my Life, hear, hear, hear me, as Thou art wont to hear Thy Chosen.

" Already, I love Thee alone, follow Thee alone, seek Thee alone, am prepared to serve Thee only, because Thou alone rulest in righteousness. O command and order what Thou wilt, but heal and open mine ears, that I may hear Thy word ; deal and open mine eyes, that I may see Thy nod ; drive out my delusion, that I may recognize Thee again. O gracious Father, take back again Thy wanderer. Have I not been chastised enough ? Have I not long enough served Thine enemies, whom Thou hast under Thy feet—long enough been the sport of deception ? Receive me as Thy servant, for I fly from those who received me as a stranger, when I fled from Thee. Increase in me faith, hope, love, according to Thy wonderful and inimitable goodness.

" I desire to come to Thee, and again implore Thee for that by which I may come. For where Thou forsakest, there is destruction ; but Thou dost not forsake, because Thou art the Highest Good, which every one, who seeks aright, will surely find. But he seeks it aright, to whom Thou hast given power to seek aright. Grant me power, O Father, to seek Thee aright ; shield me from error ! Let me not, when I seek, find another in Thy stead. I desire none other but Thee ; O let me yet find Thee, my Father ! But such a desire is vain, since Thou Thyself canst purify me and fit me to behold Thee.

"Whatever else the welfare of my mortal body may need, I commit into Thy hands, most wise and gracious Father, as long as I do not know what may be good for me, or those whom I love, and will, therefore, pray just as Thou wilt make it known at the time. Only this I beseech out of Thy great mercy, that Thou wilt convert me wholly unto Thyself, and when I obtain Thee, suffer me to be nothing else, and grant also, that, as long as I live and bear about this body, I may be pure and magnanimous, just and wise, filled with love and the knowledge of Thy wisdom, and worthy of an entrance into Thy blessed kingdom."

There are few traces of a specific churchly character in these writings. They exhibit rather a Platonism full of high thoughts, ideal views, and subtle dialectics, informed and hallowed by the spirit of Christianity. Many things were retracted by him at a later period— *e.g.*, the Platonic opinion that the human soul had a pre-existence before its present life, and that the learning of a science is a restoration of it to memory, a disinterment, so to speak, of knowledge already existing, but covered over in the mind. He had yet many steps to take before reaching the depth and clearness of Christian knowledge which distinguished his later writings, and before the new life obtained full mastery within.

After his conversion, he did indeed abandon unlawful sexual intercourse. But now the pictures of his former sensual indulgence not seldom troubled his fancy in dreams. This he regarded as sin, and reproached himself bitterly. "Am I," he cried out—"am I not then dreaming what I am, O Lord, my God ? Is not Thy

E

mighty hand able to purge all the weakness of my soul, and frighten away with more abundant grace the concupiscence of my dreams? Yea, Thou wilt grant unto me more and more Thy gifts, that my soul may follow Thee and be with Thee even in dreams full of purity; Thou, who art able to do more than we can ask or understand."

CHAPTER XVIII.

AUGUSTIN'S BAPTISM.

In the beginning of the year 387 he returned to Milan, and along with his preparation for baptism kept up his literary activity. He wished to portray the different steps of human knowledge by which he himself had been gradually led to absolute knowledge, for the purpose of leading others to the sanctuary, and wrote works on grammar, logic, rhetoric, geometry, arithmetic, philosophy, music, and on the immortality of the soul, of which only the last two were completed and have come down to us.*

Meanwhile the wished-for hour of baptism arrived. On Easter Sabbath of this year he received, at the hands of the venerable Ambrose, this holy sacrament, in company with his friend Alypius, who, as he says, always differed from him for the better, and with his son Adeodatus, who was now fifteen years of age, and, preserved

---

* The book on grammar and the principles of logic and rhetoric in the first volume of the Benedictine edition of Augustin's works is spurious, because it lacks the form of dialogue and the higher bearing which he gave to his writings on these subjects.

from the evil courses of his father, had surrendered to the Lord his youthful soul, with all its rare endowments.

This solemn act and the succeeding festivals of Easter and Whitsuntide, in which the Church entered her spiritual spring, and basked in the warm sunlight of a Saviour risen from the dead and eternally present by his Spirit, made the deepest impression upon Augustin.

The solemnity of this festival was still further heightened by two circumstances—one connected with superstition and relic-worship, the other with the effect of hymns upon the heart.

The first was the miraculous discovery of the long-concealed relics of the traditional protomartyrs of Milan, Protasius and Gervasius—two otherwise unknown Roman citizens and missionaries—who were believed to have been beheaded in the persecution of Nero or Domitian. These relics were conveyed into the Ambrosian Basilica, and, according to the current belief of that credulous age, wrought there an astonishing miracle in support of Nicene orthodoxy against the Arian heresy.*

---

* *Confess.* IX. 7 : " Then didst Thou, by a vision, discover to Thy forenamed bishop [Ambrose] where the bodies of Gervasius and Protasius, the martyrs, lay hid (whom Thou hadst in Thy secret treasury stored uncorrupted so many years), whence Thou mightest seasonably produce them to repress the fury of a woman, but an Empress [Justina]." Then Augustin relates the healing of demoniacs and of a blind man by the touch of the relics. He again refers to this noted miracle, in *De Civ. Dei* xxii. 8, as having occurred in the presence of an immense multitude. Ambrose explained it at length in a sermon, wherein he said that the Arians admitted the fact of healing, but denied the cause. Comp. his letter to his sister, Marcellina, *Ep.* xxii. (al. LIV.). These are the two authorities for the legend of the protomartyrs of Milan. The subject of post-apostolic miracles is involved in inextricable difficulties. Augustin himself is not consistent in this matter. See his opinions in Schaff's *Church History*, vol. iii., 459 sqq.

Just then, also, Ambrose had transplanted the Church-hymns of the East into his congregation, and had added to them, as the father of Latin hymnody, productions of his own, conceived and executed in a noble, liturgical style. "I could not," says Augustin, "satiate myself in those days with the wonderful delight of meditating on the depth of Thy divine counsel in the salvation of the human race. How did I weep amid Thy hymns and chants, powerfully moved by the sweetly-sounding voice of Thy Church! Those tones poured into my ear; the truth dropped into my heart, and kindled there the fire of devotion; tears ran down my cheeks in the fulness of my joy!"*

As is well known, Ambrose gets credit as the author of the magnificent anthem, *Te Deum laudamus*, which is worthy of a place among David's Psalms of thanks-giving. A mediæval tradition says that it was composed by Ambrose and Augustin jointly, during the baptism of the latter, as if by inspiration from above, each singing in response, verse after verse. But neither Ambrose nor Augustin alludes to it anywhere. The *Te Deum* is of much later date (the sixth century), though several lines can be traced to an older Greek original.

CHAPTER XIX.

MONNICA'S LAST DAYS AND DEATH.

Soon after his baptism, in the summer of the year 387, he entered on his homeward journey to Africa, in company with his relatives and friends, in order to con-

---
* *Confess.* IX. 6.

tinue there the life of divine contemplation already
begun in Cassiciacum. Among them was Evodius of
Tagaste, a cultivated man, who was baptized a short time
before, and now forsook the service of the Emperor to
live in like manner exclusively for the higher world.

Already had they reached Ostia at the mouth of the
Tiber, about a day's journey from Rome ; already had
they made the necessary preparations for embarking,
when the sudden death of Monnica frustrated the plan.
The faithful soul had now experienced the highest joy
for which she had wished to live—she had seen the
Saviour in the heart of her son, and could, like Hannah
and Simeon of old, depart in peace to that true home
which is more beautiful and sweeter far than Africa.

One day Augustin sat with his mother at a garden-
window in Ostia, and conversed with her about the rest
of eternity and its holy pleasures, which no eye has seen
and no ear heard, but which God has prepared for them
that love Him. Let us listen to his own narrative :

" Forgetting the past, and looking only toward the
future, we asked ourselves, in the presence of the Truth,
which Thou art, what the eternal life of the saints will
be. And we opened longingly the mouths of our hearts
to receive the celestial overflowings of Thy fountain, the
fountain of life, that is with Thee, that being bedewed
from it according to our capacity, we might meditate
carefully upon this solemn subject. When now our discourse had reached that point, that no pleasure of corpo-
real sense, regarded in what brilliant light soever, durst
for a moment be named with the glory of that life, much
less compared with it, we mounted upward in ardent
longing, and wandered step by step through all the material universe—the heavens, from which sun, moon, and
stars beam down upon the earth. And we rose yet

higher in inward thought, discourse, and admiration of
Thy wonderful works, and on the wings of the spirit we
rose above these also, in order to reach yon sphere of
inexhaustible fulness, where Thou dost feed Israel to all
eternity upon the pastures of Truth, where life is, and
Truth by which all was made, that was there and will
be. But truth itself was not made ; it is as it was and
always will be ; for *to have been* and *to be* are not in it,
but *being*, because it is eternal. For to *have been* and *to
be* are not eternal. While we were thus talking and desiring, we touched it gently in full rapture of heart, and
left bound there the first-fruits of the Spirit, and turned
again to the sound of our lips, where the word begins
and ends. And what is like Thy Word, our Lord, who
remains unchanged in Himself, and renews all ? We
spake thus : If the tumult of the flesh were silent, and
the images of earth, sea, and air were silent, and the
poles were silent, and the soul itself were silent, trans-
cending its own thoughts ; if dreams and the revelations
of fancy, and every language, and every sign, and everything represented by them were silent ; if all were silent,
for to him who hears, all these say, we have not made
ourselves, but He who made us dwells in eternity ; if,
at this call, they were now silent, with ear uplifted to
their Creator, and He should speak alone, not by them,
but unmediated, so that we heard *His own Word*, not
through a tongue of flesh, not through the voice of an
angel, not through the roar of thunder, not through the
dark outlines of a similitude, but from Himself, whom
we love in them, and whom, without them, we heard as
we now mounted, and with the rapid flight of thought
touched the eternal truth that lies beyond them all ; if
this contemplation should continue, and no other foreign
visions mingle with it, and if this alone should take hold

of, and absorb, and wrap up its beholder in more inward joys, and such a life as that of which, now recovering our breath, we have had a momentary taste, were to last forever, would not then the saying, ' Enter into the joy of your Lord,' be fulfilled ?' '

In the presentiment that she would soon enter into the joy of her Lord, Monnica, struck by the inspired words of her son, said : " Son, what has befallen me ? Nothing has any more charms for me in this life. What I am yet to do here, and why I am here, I do not know, every hope of this world being now consumed. Once there was a reason why I should wish to live longer, that I might see you a believing Christian * before I die. God has now richly granted me this beyond measure, in permitting me to see you in His service, having totally abandoned the world. What yet have I to do here ?"

Ary Scheffer, the French painter, of the romantic school, has fixed on this sublime moment of elevation to the beatific vision for his famous and beautiful, though somewhat sentimental picture of Monnica and her son.

> " Together 'neath the Italian heaven
> They sit, the mother and her son,
> He late from her by errors riven,
> Now both in Jesus one :
> The dear consenting hands are knit,
> And either face, as there they sit,
> Is lifted as to something seen
> Beyond the blue serene."

Five or six days after this conversation and foretaste of the eternal Sabbath-rest of the saints, the pious mother was attacked by a fever, which in a short time

---

* Or more strictly, after the original, *Confess.* IX. 10, *Christianum catholicum,* " a *Catholic* (or *orthodox*) Christian," in distinction not merely from a *Paganus,* but also and particularly from a *Christianus hæreticus* and *schismaticus,* which Augustin had formerly been.

exhausted her vital powers. Her two sons were continually at her bedside. Augustin was now indeed more than ever bowed down with grief that he had caused her so many tears and pains, and sought, by the last tender offices of love, to make as much amends as possible. Monnica read his heart, and assured him with tender affection that he had never spoken an unkind word to her. Before, it had always been her wish to die at home and rest beside the grave of her husband. But now this natural wish was merged into loftier resignation to the will of God : " Bury my body somewhere here," said she, " and do not concern yourselves on its account ; only this I beg of you, that you will be mindful of me at the altar of God, where you will be." * To the question, whether it would not be terrible to her to be buried so far from her fatherland, she replied : " Nothing is far from God ; and there is no fear that He will not know at the end of time where to raise me up."

Thus, in the fifty-sixth year of her age, on the ninth day of her sickness, this noble-hearted woman expired in the arms of her son, at the mouth of the Tiber, on the shore of the Mediterranean Sea, which separated Italy from the land of her birth. Yet, long after her death, has she consoled and comforted thousands of anxious mothers and encouraged them in patient waiting and perseverance in prayer. Her memory remains forever dear and blessed to the Christian world.†

---

* *Confess.* IX. 11 : " *Tantum illud vos rogo, ut ad Domini altare memineritis mei, ubi fueritis.*" This thanksgiving and prayer for the dead can be traced, in its innocent form, as far back as the second century, and became the fruitful germ of the doctrine of purgatory. Neither Monnica nor Augustin grasped the full meaning of St. Paul's assurance that it is " very far better to be with Christ " (Phil. i. 23).

† In an epitaph of Bassus, ex-Consul, dating from the early part of the fifth century, Monnica is addressed as " Mother of Virtues," and

Adeodatus cried aloud. Augustin himself could scarcely restrain by force the gush of tears and quiet the overpowering feelings of grief which were rushing into his heart. He believed it was not becoming "to honor such a corpse with the tearful wailings and groans which are usually given to those who die a miserable—yea, an eternal death." For his mother had not died miserably : she had merely entered into the joy of her Lord. When the weeping had subsided, his friend Evodius took up the psalter : "I will sing of mercy and judgment ; unto Thee, O Lord, will I sing" (Ps. ci. 1) ; and the whole house joined in the response.

After the corpse had been buried, and the holy Supper celebrated on the grave, according to the custom of the age, in the consciousness of a communion of saints uninterrupted by death, Augustin, finding himself at home alone with his God, gave his tears free vent, and wept sorely and long over her who had shed so many tears of maternal love and solicitude on his account. But he begs his readers to fulfil the last wish of his mother, and remember her at the altar of the Lord with thanksgiving and prayer. "In this transitory life let them remember my parents with pious affection, and my brothers, who, under Thee, the Father, are children in the mother, the Catholic Church, and my fellow-citizens in the heavenly Jerusalem, after which Thy people sigh

---

Augustin as her yet "happier offspring." This shows the early reverence paid to her memory. See the epitaph in Brieger's "Zeitschrift für Kirchengeschichte," vol. 1, p. 228. Monnica is a saint in the Roman calendar, April 4 (*Sancta Monnica vidua*). Her bones were translated from Ostia to Rome in 1430 under Pope Martin V., and deposited in a chapel dedicated to Augustin. She often appears in mediæval pictures ; especially famous is Ary Scheffer's *St. Augustin et sa mère Ste. Monique* (1845). It is in the same style as his Dante and Beatrice.

from the beginning to the end of their pilgrimage, so that what she asked of me in her last moments may be more abundantly fulfilled to her by the prayers and confessions of many, than by my prayers alone." *

These words are taken from the conclusion of the historical part of the *Confessions*, in which Augustin, with the rarest candor and in a spirit of the severest self-criticism and unfeigned humility, in presence of the whole world, acknowledges to God his sins and errors, and praises, with devout gratitude, the wonderful hand which, even in his widest wanderings, guided him, took hold of him, in the anxiety and prayers of his mother, in the better inclinations of his heart, in his internal conflicts, his increasing discontent, and his pining after God, and led him at last, after many storms, into the haven of faith and peace. In this autobiography we behold the great Church-doctor of all ages "lying in the dust of humility in converse with God and basking in the sunlight of His love, his readers only sweeping before him like shadows." He takes all his glory, all his greatness, all his culture, and lays them devoutly at the feet of free grace. His deepest feeling is—" All that is good in me is Thy ordering and Thy gift ; all that is evil is my guilt and my judgment." No motive, drawn from anything without, prompted him to this public confession. It sprang from the innermost impulse of his soul. " I believe," says he, " and therefore I speak, as Thou, Lord, knowest. Have I not confessed my guilt before Thee, and hast Thou not forgiven the sins of my soul ? Never will I excuse or justify myself before Thee, who art Truth itself ; no, I will not justify myself before Thee ; for if Thou art strict to mark iniquity, who can stand ?"

---

* *Confess.* IX. 13, conclusion.

Most touching is his sad complaint that he was converted to the Lord so late in life, since one single hour of communion with Him is worth more than all the joys of the world besides. " I have loved Thee late, whose beauty is as old as eternity, and yet so new ; I have loved Thee late. And lo ! Thou wert within, but I was without, and sought Thee there. And amid Thy beautiful creation I covered myself with loathsomeness, for Thou wert with me, and I not in Thee. The external world held me far from Thee, though it were not, if I were not in Thee. Thou didst call loud and louder, and break through my deafness ; Thou didst beam down bright and brighter, and overcome my blindness ; Thou didst breathe, and I recovered breath and life again, and breathed in Thee. I would taste Thee, and hungered and thirsted. Thou didst touch me, and, burning, I longed after Thy peace. If ever I may live in Thee, with all that is in me. then will pain and trouble leave me ; filled wholly with Thee, all within me will be life."

CHAPTER XX.

SECOND VISIT TO ROME, AND RETURN TO AFRICA.

In consequence of the death of his mother Augustin changed his plan of travel, and went, first of all, with his company to Rome, where he remained ten months.

During this time he publicly attacked his former friends, the Manichæans. He was better fitted than any one of his contemporaries for confuting their errors. " I could not," says he, in his *Retractions*, " bear in

silence that the Manichæans should delude the ignorant,
through boasting, by their false, deceptive abstemious-
ness and moderation ; and elevate themselves even above
true Christians, with whom they are not worthy to be
compared ; and so I wrote two books, the one on the
Morals of the Catholic Church, the other on the Morals
of the Manichæans."

Toward autumn of the year 388, he sailed to Africa,
and, after a transient stay in Carthage with his friend
Innocentius, a godly man, who had just then been delivered by prayer from a dangerous sickness, he proceeded
to a country-seat near Tagaste, which, along with other
real estate, he had inherited from his father. In literal
obedience to the command of Christ to the rich young
man (Matt. xix. 21), and in imitation of the example of
many saints of previous ages, he sold his possessions and
gave the proceeds to the poor, retaining, as it appears,
his dwelling and the necessary means of subsistence.

Here he lived with his friends three years in a complete community of goods, retired from the world, in
prayer, study, and meditation. He was, however, frequently interrupted by the inhabitants of the city asking
counsel about their spiritual and temporal affairs. Numerous philosophical, polemical, and theological writings
are the fruits of this sojourn in the country.

In the year 391 Augustin was called by an imperial
commissioner to the Numidian seaport, Hippo Regius,
the Bona of our time. He is yet known among the
natives of that place as "The Great Christian" (Rumi
Kebir). Hippo was destroyed by the Vandals soon after
Augustin's death. Since the French conquest of Algiers it was rebuilt, and is now one of the finest towns in
North Africa, numbering over ten thousand inhabitants—
French, Moors, and Jews. A monument was erected

to Augustin, his bronze statue on a pedestal of white marble. On the summit of the hill is a large Catholic charitable institution, where possibly may have been his garden, from which, looking out to the sea and up to heaven, he mused on "the City of God."

CHAPTER XXI.

AUGUSTIN PRIEST AND BISHOP OF HIPPO.

HAVING arrived at Hippo, he was forced into public office against his will. For, on one occasion, as he was listening to a sermon of the Bishop Valerius, a native of Greece, and the latter remarked that the congregation needed a priest, the people cried out for Augustin.

He was amazed, and burst into tears, for he did not wish to give up his peaceful, ascetic and literary retirement, and did not consider himself qualified for the responsible station. He followed, however, the guidance of that Hand which drew him, as it does every true reformer, into the arena of public life against his own inclination. He only begged for some months to prepare for the solemn office, and assumed its duties on Easter of the year 392.

His relation to the bishop was very pleasant. Valerius acknowledged the decided intellectual superiority of Augustin, and, without envy, gave it free play for the public good. He allowed him to preach frequently, contrary to the usual custom of the African bishops, who granted this privilege to the priests only during their absence. Soon after he made him an associate, with the consent of the Bishop of Carthage. But when Augustin learned the existence of a decree of the Council of Nicæa, forbidding two bishops in one congregation, he had a resolution passed by a Synod of Carthage that, in order to prevent similar irregularities, the Church canons should be read by every clergyman before ordination.

In the year 395, Valerius died, and Augustin was now sole Bishop of Hippo, and remained so till the day of his death. He says in one of his Epistles : " So exceedingly did I dread the episcopate that, because my reputation had now begun to be of some account among the servants of God, I would not go to any place where I knew there was no bishop. I did what I could that in a low place I might be saved, lest in a high one I should be perilled. But the servant must not oppose his Master. I came to this city to see a friend whom I thought I might gain to God, that he might live with us in the monastery ; I came as being safe, the place having a bishop already. I was laid hold of, made a presbyter, and by this step came to the episcopate."

In this position he was now to unfold, during a period of thirty-eight successive years, first as priest, and then as bishop, the rich treasures of his genius for the benefit of the congregation, and the whole Church in his age and all coming centuries. He was indispensable. Difficulties of deep and universal importance were arising, with which he alone was fitted to cope.

Erasmus complains that the powers of Augustin were wasted upon Africa, and thinks that he might have produced still nobler fruits in Italy or Gaul. He was mistaken. Africa presented at the time a strange mixture of native barbarism, imported civilization of the Romans, Christianity, and lingering heathenism, not unlike the present aspect of French Algiers or British East India. Aruspices still offered sacrifices. Riotous feasts of heathen idols were nominally changed into services in honor of Christian martyrs. The Christian forces were divided. The Donastist Schismatics were almost as numerous as the Catholics, and the Manichæan heretics, not to mention smaller sects, were spread over all the cities. It was no rare thing to find even in a smaller town three rival bishops—Catholic, Donatist, and Manichæan. But it was just in conflict with these antagonistic elements that Augustin's genius developed its resources ; and in contrast with the surrounding vices and signs of approaching decay his virtue and piety shine with the greater lustre. Such a man belongs to the world at large and to all ages.

CHAPTER XXII.

AUGUSTIN'S DOMESTIC LIFE.

WE will now first glance at Augustin's private life, then consider him as bishop, and lastly exhibit his public activity in the Church and the world of letters, and its influence upon succeeding generations.

His mode of living was very simple, and bore that ascetic character which accords rather with the genius of Catholicism than of Protestantism ; but it was also free from narrow bigotry and Pharisaical self-righteousness, which connect themselves so readily with monastic piety.

He dwelt with his clergy in one house, and strove with them to copy after the first community of Christians (Acts iv. 31). All things were common : no one had more than another ; even he himself was never preferred. God and His Church were enough for them.

Whoever would not consent to this was not admitted into his clerical body.

He was extremely sparing in his diet, and lived mostly on herbs and pulse. After the custom of those countries, wine was placed before all, a certain measure to each, yet of course further indulgence was severely rebuked. While they sat at table a passage from some good book was read aloud, or they conversed freely together, but were never allowed to attack the character of any one who was absent. Augustin enforced the observance of this rule of brotherly love very strictly. His clothing and house furniture were decent, without show or luxury. He was particularly prudent in regard to the female sex, for he permitted no woman, not even his nearest relative, to live in the episcopal house. Nor did he trust himself to enter into conversation with any, except in the presence of an ecclesiastic. Personally he preferred, like St. Paul and most of the Fathers, the unmarried estate (1 Cor. vii. 1, 7, 8). In this he must be judged by the ascetic standard of the early Church, which, in opposition to heathen immorality, went to the opposite extreme of an overestimate of virginity as a higher form of virtue than chastity in married life.

He also established a kind of theological seminary, where candidates could prepare themselves in a practical as well as theoretical manner, for their important duties as preachers of the Gospel. They certainly could find no better instructor. Already as a priest he had attracted to Hippo his old friends Alypius and Evodius, and several new ones, among whom were Possidius and Severus, for the prosecution of mutual studies, and these formed the beginning of that theological nursery out of which ten bishops and many inferior clergy went forth from time to time.

CHAPTER XXIII.

ADMINISTRATION OF THE EPISCOPAL OFFICE AND PUBLIC ACTIVITY.

As a bishop, Augustin was pre-eminently faithful and conscientious in the discharge of his manifold duties. He felt deeply the solemn responsibilities of the spiritual calling. "There is nothing," says he, "in this life, and especially in this age, more easy, more agreeable, and more acceptable to men than the office of bishop or presbyter or deacon, if its duties are performed at pleasure and in a time-serving spirit; but in the eyes of God nothing more miserable, more sad, more damnable. Likewise, there is nothing in this life, and especially in this age, more difficult, more laborious, more dangerous than the office of bishop or presbyter or deacon, but also more blessed before God, if a man conducts himself therein as a true soldier under the banner of Christ." [*]

To the ministry of the Word he applied himself diligently, preaching often five days in succession, and on some days twice. Whenever he found time he prepared himself for it. When, out of the fulness of inspiration he spoke from the holy place, he felt that human language was insufficient to express, in a fit and lively man-

---

[*] *Ep.* 21, tom. xi. ed. Bened. Words well worthy of being pondered on by every candidate of Theology. "*Nihil est in hac vita, et maxime hoc tempore, facilius et laetius et hominibus acceptabilius episcopi, aut presbyteri, aut diaconi officio, si perfunctorie atque adulatorie res agatur; sed nihil apud Deum miserius et tristius et damnabilius. Item nihil est in hac vita, et maxime in hoc tempore, difficilius, laboriosius, periculosius episcopi, aut presbyteri, aut diaconi officio ; sed apud Deum nihil beatius, si eo modo militetur, quo noster imperator jubet.*"

ner, the thoughts and feelings which streamed through his soul with the speed of lightning. He set before him as the aim of spiritual oratory to preach himself and his hearers into Christ, so that all might live with him and he with all in Christ. This was his passion, his honor, his boast, his joy, his riches.

He frequently spent whole days in bringing about a reconciliation between parties who were at variance. It was irksome to a man of his contemplative disposition, but a sense of duty rendered him superior to the disagreeable nature of the occupation. He speaks of " the perplexities of other people's differences in secular matters," which he was asked to decide or to adjust by mediation ; and alludes to " innumerable other ecclesiastical toils, which no one perhaps believes who has not tried." Like Ambrose, he often interceded with the authorities in behalf of the unfortunate, and procured for them either justice or mercy. He took the poor under his special care, and looked upon each clergyman as their father. Once, when he observed that but little was cast into the collection-boxes, he concluded his sermon with the words : " I am a beggar for beggars, and take pleasure in being so, in order that you may be numbered among the children of God." Like Ambrose, he even melted up the vessels of the sanctuary, in extreme cases, for the relief of the suffering and the redemption of the prisoner. Unlike many bishops of his time, he does not seem to have set his heart upon the enrichment of the Church. He would accept no legacy where injustice would be done to the natural heirs, for " the Church desires no unrighteous inheritance ;" and therefore he praised Bishop Aurelius, of Carthage, in a sermon, because he had restored, without solicitation, his entire property to a man who had willed it to the Church, and whose wife had afterward unexpectedly borne him children.

Along with his seminary for the clergy he also established religious societies for women. Over one of these his sister, a godly widow, presided. On one occasion he assured his congregation that he could not easily find better, but had also nowhere found worse people than in these cloisters.

But the activity of Augustin extended beyond the limits of his own congregation, and reached the entire African—yea, the entire Western Church. He was the leading genius of the African Synods, which were held toward the close of the fourth and the beginning of the fifth century, at Carthage, A.D. 397, 403, 411, 413, 419, and in other places, particularly against the Donatists and Pelagians. He took the liveliest interest in all the questions which were then agitated, and was unwearied in devoting his powers to the general good.

The Catholic Church had at that time three great enemies, who threatened to deface and tear her in pieces at every point, and had even forced themselves into the congregation of Hippo. These were Manichæism, Donatism, and Pelagianism. Augustin was their great opponent and final conqueror. The whole spiritual power of the Latin Church concentrated itself, so to speak, in him for the overthrow of these antagonists. He left no lawful means unemployed for the expulsion of the evil. But he principally fought with the weapon of argument, and wrote a large number of works which, although designed specially for the necessities and circumstances of the time, yet contain a store of profound truths for all ages.

CHAPTER XXIV.

LAST YEARS AND DEATH.

IN his latter years Augustin cast one more glance behind upon his entire literary course, and in his *Retractions* subjected it to a severe criticism. His writings against the Semi-Pelagians, in which a milder and more gentle spirit reigns, belong to this period. Like Luther and Melanchthon, he was inclined to melancholy with the failure of his bodily strength. This was increased by much bitter experience and the heavy misfortunes which befell his fatherland.

The Vandal king, Genseric, with fifty thousand warriors, among whom were Goths and Alani, in May of the year 428, crossed over from Spain to Africa, which was now filled with confusion and desolation. These barbarians raged more fiercely than wild beasts of prey, reduced towns and villages to ashes, spared no age or sex, were especially severe against the orthodox clergy, because they themselves were Arians, and changed that beautiful country into a desert.

Augustin was of the opinion that the bishops at least should stand by their congregations in the hour of need, that the bonds which the love of Christ had knit should not be rent asunder, and that they should endure quietly whatever God might send. "Whoever flies," he wrote to Bishop Quodvultdeus, "so that the Church is not deprived of the necessary ministrations, he does what God commands or permits. But whoever so flies that the flock of Christ is left without the nourishment by which it spiritually lives, he is an hireling, who, seeing the wolf come, flies because he has no care for the sheep."

Boniface, the commander-in-chief of the imperial forces in Africa, who was friendly to Augustin, though the occasion of much trouble to him, was beaten by the Vandals, and threw himself with the remnant of his army into the fortified city of Hippo, where Possidius and several other bishops had taken refuge. Augustin was sorely oppressed by the calamities of his country and the destruction of divine worship, which could now be celebrated only in the strongholds of Carthage, Cirta, and Hippo. At table he once expressed himself to his friends in the following language : "What I pray God for is that He will deliver this city from the enemy, or if He has determined otherwise, that He may strengthen His servant for his sufferings, or, which I would rather, that He will call me from this world to Himself."

The last wish was granted him. In the third month of the siege he was attacked by a violent fever, and ten days before his death he withdrew into retirement, after having, up till that time, proclaimed the Word of God to his congregation without interruption. He spent this season in reading the penitential psalms, which were attached to the wall by his bedside, in holy meditations, tears, prayers, and intercessions. He once said that no one, especially no priest, ought to depart this life without earnest repentance, and wrote concerning himself : " I will not cease to weep until He comes, and I appear before Him, and these tears are to me pleasant nutriment. The thirst which consumes me, and incessantly draws me toward yon fountain of my life—this thirst is always more burning when I see my salvation delayed. This inextinguishable desire carries me away to those streams, as well amid the joys as amid the sorrows of this world. Yea, if I stand well with the world I am wretched in myself, until I appear before God."

On the 28th of August, 430, in the seventy-sixth year of his age, the great man peacefully departed into a blissful eternity, in the full possession of his faculties, and in the presence of his friends.

He left no will, for, having embraced voluntary poverty, he had nothing to dispose of, except his books and manuscripts, which he bequeathed to the Church.*

Soon after Hippo was taken. Henceforth Africa was lost to the Romans, and vanished from the arena of Church History. The culminating point of the spiritual greatness of the African Church was also that of her ruin. But her ripest fruit, the spirit and the theology of Augustin, could not perish. It fell on the soil of Europe, where it has produced new glorious flowers and fruits, and to this day exerts a mighty influence in Catholic and Protestant Christendom.

CHAPTER XXV.

AUGUSTIN'S WRITINGS.

AUGUSTIN is the most fruitful author among the Latin Church-Fathers. His writings are almost too numerous. One of his biographers reckons them, including about four hundred sermons and two hundred and seventy letters, at ten hundred and thirty. Others reduce the whole

---

* His friend and biographer, Possidius, says, *Vit. Aug.* c. 31 : " *Testamentum nullum fecit, quia unde faceret, pauper Dei non habuit. Ecclesiæ bibliothecam omnesque codices diligenter posteris custodiendos semper jubebat.*"

number to two hundred and thirty-two, and the larger ones to ninety-three. They fill eleven folio volumes in the Benedictine edition of Augustin's works.*

They contain his views in every department of theology, the rare treasures of his mind and heart, and a true expression of the deepest religious and churchly movements of his age, and at the same time secured an immeasurable influence upon all succeeding generations. He wrote out of the abundance of his heart, not to acquire literary fame, but moved by the love of God and man.

In point of learning he stands far behind Origen, Eusebius, and Jerome ; but in originality, depth, and wealth of thought he surpasses all the Greek and Latin Fathers. He knew no Hebrew and very little Greek, as he modestly confesses himself.† He neglected and disliked the noble language of Hellas in his youth, because he had a bad teacher, and was forced to it. But after his conversion, during his second residence in Rome, he resumed the study of it, and acquired a sufficient elementary knowledge to compare the Latin version of the Scriptures with the Septuagint and the Greek Testament.‡

---

* A considerable number of them have been translated into English, especially the *Confessions*, the *City of God*, and the Homilies on the Psalms, and St. John. See the Oxford " Library of the Fathers," 1837 sqq., and Clark's edition of the " Works of Aurelius Augustine," ed. by Marcus Dods, D.D., Edinburgh 1871–1876, 15 vols. 8vo.

† " *Græcæ linguæ perparum assecutus sum, et prope nihil.*" *Contra Literas Petiliani* II. 38. Comp. *De Trinitate* III. Prooem.; *Confess.* I. 14 ; VII. 9.

‡ He gives the etymology of several Greek words, as αἰώνιον, ἀνάθεμα, ἐγκαίνια, λόγος, etc. ; he correctly distinguishes between γεννᾶν and τίκτειν, ἐνταφιάζειν and θάπτειν, εὐχή and προσευχή, πνοή and πνεῦμα. He amends the *Itala* in about thirty places from the Septuagint, and in three places from the Greek Testament (John

Gibbon, usually very accurate, underestimates him when he says that "the superficial learning of Augustin was confined to the Latin language," and that "his style, though sometimes animated by the eloquence of passion, is usually clouded by false and affected rhetoric."* The judgment of Dr. Baur, who had as little sympathy with Augustin's theology, but a far better knowledge of it, is more just and correct : "There is scarcely another theological author so fertile and withal so able as Augustin. His scholarship was certainly not equal to his genius ; yet even that is sometimes set too low, when it is asserted that he had no acquaintance at all with the Greek language ; for this is incorrect, though he had attained no great proficiency in Greek." †

---

viii. 25 ; xviii. 37 ; Rom. i. 3). He also corrects Julian, his Pelagian antagonist, by going back to the Greek. He explains the Greek monogram ἰχϑύς (De Civ. Dei xviii. 23). He mentions the opinion (De Civ. Dei xx. 19) that in 2 Thess. ii. 4 we should render the Greek (εἰς τὸν ναὸν τοῦ ϑεοῦ), not in templo Dei, but more correctly in templum Dei, as if Antichrist and his followers were themselves the temple of God, the Church. He probably read Plotinus and Porphyry in the original. Comp. Loesche : De Augustino Plotinizante in doctrina de Deo, Jena, 1880.

* Decline and Fall, Ch. XXXIII. He adds that "Augustin possessed a strong, capacious, argumentative mind ; he boldly sounded the abyss of grace, predestination, free will, and original sin ; and the rigid system of Christianity which he framed or restored has been entertained with public applause and secret reluctance by the Catholic Church." He says in a note : "The Church of Rome has canonized Augustin and reprobated Calvin."

† Dogmengesch. I. 1, p. 61 ; comp. the section on Augustin in the second volume of Baur's Church History. Compare also the judgments of Villemain, Tableau de l'éloquence chrétienne au IVe siècle, Paris, 1849, p. 373 ; of Ozanam, La civilization au cinquième siècle (vol. I. 272, in Glyn's translation) ; and the eloquent account of the veteran and liberal historian, Karl Hase, in the first volume of his Lectures on Church History, Leipzig, 1885, vol. I. 514 sqq.

His style may indeed be blamed for verbosity, negligence, and frequent repetition, but he says : " I would rather be censured by the grammarians than not understood by the people ;" and, upon the whole, he had the language wholly at command, and knew how to wield the majestic power, the dignity and music of the Latin in a masterly manner. His writings are full of ingenious puns, and rise not seldom to strains of true eloquence and poetic beauty. Several of his pregnant sentences have become permanently lodged in the memory of the Christian world. Such words of genius and wisdom engraven upon the rock are worth more than whole libraries written upon the sand. The following are among his most striking and suggestive thoughts :

Cor nostrum inquietum est donec requiescat in Te.
Our heart is restless until it rests in Thee.
Novum Testamentum in Vetere latet, Vetus in Novo patet.
The New Testament is concealed in the Old, the Old is revealed in the New.
Ubi amor ibi trinitas.
Where love is there is trinity.
Distingue tempora, et concordabit Scriptura.
Distinguish the times, and the Scriptures will agree.
Da quod jubes, et jube quod vis.
Give what Thou commandest, and command what Thou wilt.
Fides præcedit intellectum.
Faith precedes knowledge.
Non vincit nisi veritas ; victoria veritatis est caritas.
Truth only is victorious ; the victory of truth is charity.
Nulla infelicitas frangit, quem felicitas nulla corrumpit.
No misfortune can break him whom no fortune corrupts.
Deo servire vera libertas est.
To serve God is true liberty.

To Augustin is also popularly but falsely ascribed the famous and beautiful device of Christian union :

In necessariis unitas, in dubiis libertas, in omnibus caritas.
In essentials unity, in non-essentials liberty, in all things charity.

This sentence cannot be found in his writings. It is too liberal for a Catholic divine, and is probably of Protestant origin. It has been traced to Rupert Meldenius and Richard Baxter, two irenical divines of the seventeenth century, one a German Lutheran or Melanchthonian, the other an English Presbyterian, who in the midst of the fury of theological controversies grew sick of strife and longed after union and peace.

Since his productive period as an author extends over four decades of years, from his conversion to the evening of his life, and since he unfolded himself before the eyes of the public, contradictions on many minor points were unavoidable; wherefore, in old age, he subjected his literary career to a conscientious revision in his *Retractions*, and, in a spirit of genuine Christian humility, recalled much that he had maintained before from honest conviction. But not all his changes are improvements. He had more liberal views in his younger years.

His philosophical writings, which were composed soon after his conversion, and which are yet full of Platonism, we have already mentioned.

His theological works may be divided into five classes :*

1. EXEGETICAL Writings. Here we may name his Expositions of the Sermon on the Mount (393), of the Epistle to the Galatians (394), of the Psalms (415), of John (416), his Harmony of the Gospels (400), and an extensive commentary on the first three chapters of Genesis (415).

His strength lies not in knowledge of the original lan-

---

* For a fuller account see the author's *Church History*, vol. III. (revised ed. 1884), p. 1005 sqq. For his philosophical works and opinions the reader is referred to Ritter, Erdmann, Ueberweg, Nourrison, Gangauf, and A. Dorner, mentioned there, p. 989 and 1039.

guages, nor in historical and grammatical exegesis, in which he was excelled by Jerome among the Latins, and Chrysostom, Theodoret, and Theophylact among the Greeks, but in the development of theological and religious thought. He depended mostly on the imperfect *Itala*, which was current before Jerome's Vulgate. Hence he often misses the natural sense. But he had an uncommon familiarity and full inward sympathy with the Holy Scriptures, and often penetrates their deepest meaning by spiritual intuition. He is ingenious and suggestive, even where he violates the grammar or loses himself in allegorical fancies. He exercised also a considerable influence on the final settlement of the canon of Holy Scripture, whose limit was so firmly fixed at the Synods of Hippo in the year 393, and of Carthage in 397, that even now it is universally received in the Catholic and Evangelical churches, with the exception of a difference in regard to the value of the Old Testament Apocrypha, which the Council of Trent included in the Canon, while the Protestant Confessions exclude them or assign them a subordinate position.

2. APOLOGETIC Writings. To these belong pre-eminently his twenty-two books on the " City of God " (*De Civitate Dei*), begun in 413 and finished in 426, in the seventy-second year of his life. It is his most learned and influential work. It is a noble and genial defence of Christianity and the Church, in the face of the approaching downfall of the old Roman Empire and classic civilization, in the face of the irruption of the wild, northern barbarians into Southern Europe and Africa, and in the face of the innumerable misfortunes and calamities by which the human race was scourged during that transition-period, and which were attributed by the heathen to the decay of the ancient faith in the gods,

and laid to the charge of Christianity. Augustin shows that all these events are the result of a process of internal putrefaction long since begun, a judgment to the heathen, and a powerful call on them to awake and repent, and at the same time a healthful trial to Christians, and the birth-throes of a new spiritual creation. Then he turns from the view of a perishing natural world and her representative, the city of Rome, conquered and laid waste by Alaric, the King of the Goths, in the year 410, to the contemplation of a higher, supernatural world—to the City of God, founded by Christ upon a rock ; this city can never be destroyed, but out of all the changes and revolutions of time must rise, phœnix-like, with new power and energy ; and after the fulfilment of her earthly mission shall be separated even from external communion with the world, and enter into the Sabbath of eternal rest and spiritual repose. " The City of God " is the first attempt at a philosophy of history, viewed under the aspect of two antagonistic kingdoms.

3. DOGMATIC and POLEMIC Works. These are very numerous and important. Augustin was particularly endowed as a speculative divine, a powerful reasoner, and an acute controversialist. There is scarcely a theological question which he did not revolve in his mind over and over again. He ascended the highest heights and sounded the deepest depths of religious speculation. His opinions are always worth considering. He had very strong convictions, but was free from passion, and never indulged in personalities. He was forcible in matter and sweet in spirit, and spoke " the truth in love."

Among his dogmatic works we mention the fifteen books on the Holy Trinity (against the Arians) ; the hand-book (*Enchiridion*) on Faith, Hope, and Love ; and the four books on Christian doctrine (*De Doctrina*

Christiana), a hermeneutic dogmatic compendium for religious teachers, and instruction in the development of Christian doctrine from the Holy Scripture.

His polemic treatises may again be divided into three classes :

(*a*) *Anti-Manichæan* Writings : "On the Morals of the Manichæans ;" on the "Morals of the Catholic Church ;" on "Free Will ;" on the "Two Souls ;" "Against Faustus," and others. They are the chief source of our knowledge of the Manichæan errors, and their refutation. They belong to his earliest works. They defend the freedom of will against fatalism ; afterwards he changed his opinion on that subject.

(*b*) *Anti-Donatistic* Writings : "On Baptism against the Donatists ;" "Against the Epistle of Parmenianus ;" "Against Petilianus ;" "Extract from the Transactions of the Religious Conference with the Donatists ;" and others. They are the chief source of our knowledge of the remarkable Donatistic schism in Africa, which began long before Augustin's time, and was overcome principally by his intellectual ability. They treat chiefly of the essence and the attributes of the Church and her relation to the world, of the evil of schism and separation. They complete the development of the Catholic idea of the Church, her visible unity and universality, which was begun already by Ignatius and Irenæus, and carried on by Cyprian. They were composed between 393 and 420.

Unfortunately he approved also of coercive measures of state for the suppression of the separatistic movement, and supported it by a false exegesis of the passage, "Compel them to come in" (Luke xiv. 23). He thus furnished the chief authority in the middle ages for those cruel persecutions of heretics which blacken so many

pages of Church History, and from which, if he could
have foreseen them, his own Christian feelings would
have shrunk back in horror. Thus great and good men,
even without intending it, have, through mistaken zeal,
occasioned much mischief.

(c) *Anti-Pelagian* Writings, of the years 411–420, to
which are to be added the *anti-Semi-Pelagian* writings
of the last years of his life. We mention here the books
"On Nature and Grace;" "On Merit and Forgiveness;" "On Grace and Free-Will;" "On the Spirit
and the Letter;" "On Original Sin;" "On the Predestination of the Saints;" "On the Gift of Perseverance" (*De Dono Perseverantiæ*); "Against Pelagius
and Cœlestius;" "Against Julian" (a bishop of Eclanum
in Apulia, infected with Pelagianism). In these treatises
Augustin develops his profound doctrines of original sin,
the natural inability of man for good; of the grace and
merit of Christ; of eternal election; of faith and perseverance to the end—in opposition to the shallow and
superficial errors of the contemporaneous monks, Pelagius and Cœlestius, who denied natural depravity, and
just so far overthrew the value of divine grace in Christ.

These books belong to his most meritorious labors, and
are decidedly evangelical, though not free from exaggerations. They have exerted a greater influence on the
Reformers of the sixteenth century, especially on Luther,
Melanchthon, and Calvin, than any of his own or of all
other human productions besides.* His anti-Pelagian
views of sin and grace and divine forecordination are
technically called "the Augustinian system," and this

---

* I furnished a detailed representation of the Pelagian controversy
and Augustin's views in connection with it for the "Bibliotheca
Sacra and Theological Review" of Andover for the year 1848, vol. v.,
p. 205–243, and in my *Church History*, vol. III., 783–865.

again is often, though erroneously, identified with the Calvinistic system of theology. But he held along with it other views which are essentially Catholic and unprotestant, especially on the Church, on baptism, on justification, on asceticism.

4. ASCETIC and PRACTICAL Writings. Among these we may number the "Soliloquies;" "Meditations;" "On the Christian Conflict;" "On the Excellency of Marriage," and a great mass of sermons and homilies, part of which were written out by himself and part taken down by his hearers. Of these there are about four hundred, besides those which that indefatigable editor of unpublished manuscripts, Cardinal Angelo Mai, has discovered among the treasures of the Vatican Library, and given to the press.

5. AUTOBIOGRAPHICAL, or writings which concern his own life and personal relations. Here belong the invaluable "Confessions," already known to us—his exhibition of himself to the time of his conversion ; the "Retractions," his revision and self-correcting retrospect at the close of his splendid career in the Church and the fields of literature ; lastly, a collection of two hundred and seventy letters, in which he exhibits a true picture of his external and internal life.

CHAPTER XXVI.

From this comprehensive mass of writings it is easy to
determine the significance and influence of Augustin.

In the sphere of theology, as well as in all other
spheres of literature, it is not the quantity, but the qual-
ity of the intellectual product which renders it most
effective.   The apostles have written but little ; and
yet the Gospel of St. John, for example, or the Epistle
to the Romans exert more influence than whole libraries
of excellent books—yea, than the literatures of whole
nations.   Tertullian's "Apology ;" Cyprian's short
treatise on the "Unity of the Church ;" Anselm's "Cur
Deus homo," and "Monologium ;" Bernhard's tracts on
"Despising the World," and on "The Love of God ;"
the anonymous little book of "German Theology," and
similar productions, which may be contained in a couple
of sheets, have moved and blessed more minds than the
numerous abstruse folio volumes of many scholastics of
the Middle Ages and old Protestant divines.   Augustin's
"Confessions ;" the simple little book of the humble,
secluded monk, Thomas à Kempis, on the "Imitation
of Christ ;" Bunyan's "Pilgrim's Progress ;" Arndt's
"True Christianity," have each converted, edified,
strengthened, and consoled more persons than whole
ship-loads of indifferent religious books and commentaries.

But Augustin was not only a voluminous writer, but also
a profound thinker and subtle reasoner.   His books, with
all the faults and repetitions of isolated parts, are a spon-

taneous outflow from the marvellous treasures of his highly-gifted mind and his truly pious heart. Although he occupied one of the smaller bishoprics, he was yet, in fact, the head and leading spirit of the African Church, around whom Aurelius of Carthage, the primate of Africa, Evodius of Uzala, Fortunatus of Cirta, Possidius of Calama, Alypius of Tagaste, and many other bishops willingly and gladly ranged themselves—yea, in him the whole Western Church of antiquity reached its highest spiritual vigor and bloom. His appearance in the history of dogmas forms a distinct epoch, especially as it regards anthropological and soteriological doctrines, which he advanced considerably further, and brought to a greater clearness and precision than they had ever had before in the consciousness of the Church. For this was needed such a rare union of the speculative talent of the Greek, and of the practical spirit of the Latin Church as he alone possessed. As in the doctrines of sin and grace, of the fall of Adam and the redemption of Christ, the two cardinal points of practical Christianity, he went far beyond the theology of the Oriental Church, which devoted its chief energies to the development of the dogmas of the Holy Trinity and the person of Christ, so at the same time he opened up new paths for the progress of Western theology.

Not only over his own age, but over all succeeding generations also, he has exercised an immeasurable influence, and does still, as far as the Christian Church and theological science reach, with the exception of the Greek Church, which adheres to her own traditions and the decisions of the seven Œcumenical Councils. It may be doubted if ever any uninspired theologian has had and still has so large a number of admirers and disciples as the Bishop of Hippo. While most of the great

G

men in the history of the Church are claimed either by the Catholic or by the Protestant Confession, and their influence is therefore confined to one or the other, he enjoys from both a respect equally profound and enduring.

On the one hand, he is among the chief creators of the *Catholic* theology. Through the whole of the Middle Ages, from Gregory the Great down to the Fathers of Trent, he was the highest theological authority. Thomas Aquinas alone could in some measure contest this rank with him. By his fondness for speculation and his dialectic acumen he became the father of mediæval *scholasticism;* and at the same time, by his devotional fervor and spirit glowing with love, the author of mediæval *mysticism.* Hence the most distinguished representatives of scholasticism—as Anselm, Peter Lombard, Thomas Aquinas—and the representatives of mysticism—as Bernhard of Clairvaux, Hugo of St. Victor, and Tauler—have collectively appealed to his authority, been nourished on his writings, and saturated with his spirit. Even at this day the Catholic Church, notwithstanding her condemnation of many doctrines of Augustin, under the names of Protestant, and Jansenist heresies, counts him among her greatest saints and most illustrious doctors.

It must not be omitted that he is responsible also for many grievous errors of the Roman Church. He advocated the principle of persecution ; he taught the damnation of unbaptized infants ; he anticipated the dogma of the immaculate conception of the Virgin Mary ; and his ominous word, *Roma locuta est, causa finita est,* might almost be quoted in favor of the Vatican decree of papal infallibility. These errors lie like an incubus on the Roman Church. Error is all the more tenacious and dangerous the greater the truth it contains, and the greater and wiser the man who advocates it.

But, on the other hand, this same Augustin has also an *evangelical-Protestant* significance. Next to the Apostle Paul, he was the chief teacher of the whole body of the Reformers of the sixteenth century, and his exegetical and anti-Pelagian writings were the main source from which they derived their views on the depravity of human nature and the excellence of the forgiving, regenerating, and sanctifying grace of God in Christ, and opposed the dead formalism, self-righteous Pelagianism, and stiff mechanism of the scholastic theology and monkish piety of that age. As is well known, they followed him from the very beginning even to the dizzy abyss of the doctrine of predestination, which Luther (in his work *De Servo Arbitrio*) and Calvin reproduced in its most rigorous form, in order to root out Pelagianism and Semi-Pelagianism, and with them all human boasting. Of Augustin they always speak with high esteem and love, which is the more remarkable because they are otherwise very free not only with the mediæval schoolmen, but with the ancient Fathers, and sometimes even, in the passionate heat of their opposition to slavish reverence, treat them with neglect and contempt.*

---

* In this, as everywhere, Luther is especially outspoken and characteristic. His contempt for Scholasticism, which he derives from "the accursed heathen Aristotle," is well known. Even the writings of Thomas Aquinas, for whom the Lutheran theologians of the seventeenth century had great respect, he once calls "the dregs of all heresies, error, and destruction of the Gospel." Neither did he spare the ancient Fathers, being conscious of the difference between Protestant and Patristic theology. "All the Fathers," he once says without ceremony, "have erred in faith, and, if not converted before death, are eternally damned." "St. Gregory is the useless fountainhead and author of the fables of purgatory and masses for souls. He

I will add the most recent estimates of Augustin by
Protestant historians in confirmation of the views expressed in this chapter.

---

was very ill acquainted with Christ and His Gospel ; he is entirely
too superstitious ; the Devil has corrupted him." On Jerome, whose
Vulgata was indispensable in his translation of the Bible into German, he was particularly severe on account of his monastic tendencies and legalism. He calls him a "heretic who has written much
profanity. He has deserved hell more than heaven. I know no one
of the Fathers to whom I am so hostile, as to him. He writes only
about fasting, virginity, and such things." For the same reason he
condemns St. Basil, one of the chief promoters of monachism :
" He is good for nothing ; is only a monk ; I would not give a straw
for him." Of Chrysostom, the greatest expounder of the Scriptures
and pulpit-orator of the Greek Church, but of whom certainly he had
only the most superficial knowledge, he says, " He is worth nothing
to me ; he is a babbler, wrote many books, which make a great show,
but are only huge, wild, tangled heaps and crowds and bags full of
words, for there is nothing in them, and little wool sticks." Nowadays not a solitary Lutheran theologian of any learning will agree
with him in this view. The Reformer was at times dissatisfied with
Augustin himself, because, amid all his congeniality of mind, he
could not just find in him his " *sola* fide." " Augustin has often
erred, he is not to be trusted. Although good and holy, he was yet
lacking in true faith as well as the other Fathers." But over against
this casual expression stand a number of eulogies on Augustin.

Luther's words must not be weighed too nicely, else any and everything can be proven by him, and the most irreconcilable contradictions shown. We must always judge him according to the moment
and mood in which he spoke, and duly remember his bluntness and
his stormy, warlike nature. Thus, the above disparaging sentences
upon some of the greatest theologians are partly annulled by his
churchly and historical feeling, and by many expressions, like that
in a letter to Albert of Prussia (A.D. 1532), where he declares the importance of tradition in matters of faith, as strongly as any Catholic.
In reference to the real presence of Christ in the Lord's Supper, he
says : " Moreover this article has been unanimously believed and
held from the beginning of the Christian Church to the present
hour, as may be shown from the books and writings of the dear
Fathers, both in the Greek and Latin languages, which testimony

Dr. Bindemann, one of the best Protestant biographers of Augustin, thus sums up his estimate of his character and influence : "Augustin is one of the most extraordinary lights in the Church. In importance he takes rank behind no teacher who has labored in her since the days of the apostles. It may well be said that the first place among the Church Fathers is due to him, and at the time of the Reformers only a Luther, by reason of the fulness and depth of his spirit and his nobleness of character, was worthy to stand at his side. He is the highest point of the development of the Western Church before the Middle Ages. From him the Mysticism, no less than the Scholasticism of the Middle Ages, has drawn its life ; he forms the mightiest pillar of Roman Catholicism ; and the leaders of the Reformation derived from his writings next to the study of the Holy Scriptures, especially the Paulinian Epistles, those principles which gave birth to a new era." Dr. Kurtz (in the ninth edition of his *Church History*, 1885) calls Augustin "the greatest, mightiest, and most influential of all the fathers, from whom the entire doctrinal and ecclesiastical development of the Occident proceeded, and to whom it returns again and again in all its turning-points." Dr. Carl

of the entire holy Christian Church ought to be sufficient for us, even if we had nothing more. *For it is dangerous and dreadful to hear or believe anything against the unanimous testimony, faith, and doctrine of the entire holy Christian Church, as it has been held unanimously in all the world up to this year* 1500. Whoever now doubts of this, he does just as much as though he believed in no Christian Church, and condemns not only the entire holy Christian Church as a damnable heresy, but Christ Himself, and all the apostles and prophets, who founded this article, when we say, 'I believe in a holy Christian Church,' to which Christ bears powerful testimony in Matt. xxviii. 20 : ' Lo I am with you always to the end of the world,' and Paul in 1 Tim. iii. 15 : ' The Church is the pillar and ground of the truth.' "

Burk (in his *Church History*, 1885) says that in Augustin ancient and modern ideas are melted, and that to his authority the papal church has as much right to appeal as the churches of the Reformation. Dr. Karl Hase, of Jena, who, after lecturing on Church History from 1831 to 1883, is now (1885) publishing his lectures, emphasizes the liberal features of Augustin, and remarks that "a right estimate of his importance as an author can only be made when we perceive how the scholastics and mystics of the Middle Ages lived upon his riches, and how even Luther and Calvin drew out of his depths."

The great genius of the African Church, from whom the Middle Ages and the Reformation have received an impulse alike powerful, though in different directions, has not yet fulfilled the work marked out for it in the counsels of Divine Wisdom. He serves as a bond of union between the two antagonistic sections of Western Christendom, and encourages the hope that a time may come when the injustice and bitterness of strife will be forgiven and forgotten, and the discords of the past be drowned forever in the sweet harmonies of perfect knowledge and perfect love.

This end may be afar off. It will come when the "City of God" is completed. "Then and there" (to use the closing words of his admirable work) "we shall rest and see, see and love, love and praise. This is what shall be in the end without end. For what other end do we propose to ourselves than to attain to the Kingdom of which there shall be no end?"

What Augustin has so beautifully said of men as individuals may, with great propriety, be applied also to the ages of the Church : "Thou, O Lord, hast created us for Thyself, and our hearts are without rest until they rest in Thee."

CHAPTER XXVII.

THE AUGUSTINIAN SYSTEM.

A FEW words more on the anti-Pelagian system of Augustin, which is so closely interwoven with the history of Protestant theology. . It is imbedded in the Confessions of the Reformation ; it ruled the scholastic theology of the Lutheran and Reformed churches during the seventeenth century ; it was gradually undermined first by the Arminian movement in Holland, then by the Wesleyan Methodism in England and America, and by the rationalistic revolution of the last century, but is still held by the schools of strict orthodoxy in the Lutheran and Calvinistic churches, with this difference, however, that the Lutheran Formula of Concord teaches a *universal call* in connection with a *particular election*, and rejects the decree of reprobation.

The Roman Church accepted Augustinianism only in part and in subordination to her sacramentarian and sacerdotal system. The Greek Church ignored it altogether, although Pelagius was condemned with Nestorius by the Œcumenical Council of Ephesus in 431, without a doctrinal statement of the controverted points.

The Augustinian system assumes but one probation of man and but one act of freedom, which was followed by a universal slavery of sin and by a partial redemption ; God choosing by an eternal decree of grace from the mass of perdition a definite number of the elect for salvation, and leaving the rest to their deserved ruin. It suspends the eternal fate of Adam and his unborn posterity, which he represented, upon a single act of disobedience, which resulted in the damnation of untold millions of immortal beings, including all unbaptized infants dying in infancy. That act, with its fearful consequences, was, of course, eternally foreseen by the omniscient God, and must in some sense also have been decreed or foreordained, since nothing can happen without His sovereign and almighty will. Augustin and the Protestant Confessions stop within the *infralapsarian* scheme, which puts the fall only under a *permissive* decree, and makes Adam and the race responsible for sin. Here is an inconsistency, which has its root in a strong sense of God's holiness and man's guilt. The *supralapsarian* scheme, which was developed by a school in Calvinistic churches, but never obtained symbolical sanction, is logically more consistent, but practically more revolting by including the fall itself in an *efficient* decree of God, and making sin the necessary means for the manifestation of divine mercy in the saved, and of divine justice in the lost.

Melanchthon in his later years, and the Arminians after him, felt the speculative and moral difficulties of Augustinianism, but were no more able to remove them by their compromise theories than the Semi-Pelagians of old. Yea, even Calvin, while accepting in faith the absolute decree, called it a "*decretum horribile, attamen verum.*"

Long before Augustin, Origen had taught another solution of the problem of sin, based on the Platonic theory of pre-existence ; he went even beyond the beginning of history where Augustin began, and assumed a *pre-historic* fall of every individual soul (not of the race, as Augustin held), but also a final salvation of all.

Schleiermacher combined the Augustinian or Calvinistic predestinarianism with the Origenistic restorationism, and taught a universal election, which unfolds itself by degrees, and, while involving a *temporary* reprobation of the impenitent, results in the final conversion and restoration of all men to holiness and happiness. Pantheism goes still further, and makes sin a necessary transition point in the process of moral evolution, but thereby cuts the nerve of moral responsibility, and overthrows the holiness of God.

Thus the deepest and strongest minds, both philosophers and theologians, have been wrestling again and again with the dark, terrific problem of sin and death in its relation to an all-wise, holy, and merciful God, and yet have reached no satisfactory solution except that God overrules evil for a greater good. The Augustinian system contains a vast amount of profound truth, and has trained some of the purest and strongest types of Christian character among the Jansenists and Huguenots of France, the Calvinists of Holland, the Puritans of England, the Covenanters of Scotland, and the Pilgrim Fathers of New England. Nevertheless, as a system it is unsatisfactory, because it assumes an unconscious and yet responsible pre-existence of the race in Adam, and because it leaves out of sight the *universal* benevolence and *impartial* justice of God to all His creatures, and the freedom and individual responsibility of man, who stands or falls with his own actual sins. But it will require another theological genius even deeper and broader than Origen, Augustin, Thomas Aquinas, Calvin, and Schleiermacher, to break the spell of that system by substituting a better one from the inexhaustible mines of the Scripture, which contains all the elements and aspects of the truth, without giving disproportion to one and doing injustice to another.

The study of history liberalizes and expands the mind, and teaches us to respect and love, without idolatry, every great and good man notwithstanding his errors of judgment and defects of character. There never was an unerring and perfect being on earth but One who is more than man, and who alone could say : " I am the Way, and the Truth, and the Life."

P.S.—This biography is an enlarged revision of the author's *St. Augustin*, which was published in German by W. Hertz, in Berlin, 1854, and admirably translated by his friend, Professor Thomas C. Porter (New York, and London, Samuel Bagster & Sons, 1854), but has long since been out of print. The changes and additions are considerable, but the popular character and aim have been retained.

MELANCHTHON.

HIS YOUTH AND EDUCATION.

PHILIP MELANCHTHON, the second leader of the German Reformation and the " Teacher of Germany" (*Præceptor Germaniæ*), was born of honest and pious parents, February 16th, 1497, fourteen years after Luther, at Bretten, in the beautiful and fertile Palatinate, now belonging to the Grand Duchy of Baden.

His parents were in comfortable circumstances, and had five children, Philip being the oldest. His father, Georg Schwarzerd, was a manufacturer of arms for the Elector Philip of the Palatinate, and formerly resided at Heidelberg. He once made a skilfully contrived armor for the Emperor Maximilian I., in which this last of the mediæval knights conquered a bold Italian in a tournament. Melanchthon himself afterward prepared the spiritual weapons for the conflict of Germany with the Pope of Rome. His mother, Barbara Reuter, is described as a prudent, economical, and benevolent woman. She was a niece of the celebrated classical and Hebrew scholar John Reuchlin, of Pforzheim, who suffered much persecution from ignorant Dominican monks for promoting Biblical learning.*

---

* See Förstemann, *Die Schwarzerde, oder Zusammenstellung der Nachrichten über Melanchthon's Geschlecht*, in the " Theol. Studien und Kritiken," 1830, p. 119 sqq. Also Carl Schmidt, *Philipp Melanchthon*, Elberfeld, 1861, p. 1–6.

Melanchthon lost his father in early boyhood, but Reuchlin took charge of his education, gave him, according to the literary fashion of the age, his Greek name *Melanchthon*, or *Melanthon*,* in exchange for the German family name *Schwarzerd* (*Black-earth*), together with the rare and costly present of a Latin Bible, and sent him to the Latin school at Pforzheim (1507), and to the Universities of Heidelberg (1509) and Tübingen (1512).

He studied philosophy, mathematics, natural science, law, and medicine, but especially the Greek and Roman classics, which were then raised to life again after a long sleep in the dust of ages, and which kindled the fire of enthusiasm for liberal culture among scholars in Italy, France, England, Holland, and Germany. It was an age of literary discovery preparatory to the Reformation, and in many respects resembles our own age of restless progress. It was the century of the Renaissance, when the world and the Church renewed their youth. "The studies flourish," said Ulrich von Hutten, "the spirits are awake, it is a luxury to live." And Luther wrote in 1522 : "If you read all the annals of the past, you will find no century like this since the birth of Christ. Such building and planting, such good living and dressing, such enterprise in commerce, such stir in all the arts, has not been since Christ came into the world. And how numerous are the sharp and intelligent wits who leave nothing hidden and unturned ! Even a boy of twenty years knows more nowadays than was formerly known by twenty doctors of divinity."

---

* He spelled his name *Melanchthon* till 1531 ; afterward he adopted the shorter form, for easier pronunciation. In the University of Heidelberg he was immatriculated as " *Philippus Schwarzerd de Bretten.*" The Greek name is from μέλαν, *black*, and χθών, *earth*.

In theology Melanchthon had at that time less interest, as it was taught in the dry, barren method of mediæval scholasticism in the last stages of dissolution ; but he had received a pious training at home, and took great delight in public worship, and in reading the Greek Testament, and the lives of saints.

By the extraordinary precocity of his genius, in connection with great modesty and amiability of character, he attracted favorable attention, and rose with unexampled rapidity to the highest rank of classical and general scholarship. He wrote and spoke the ancient languages better than his native German. He composed poetry in Latin and Greek. He learned the Hebrew from Reuchlin's Grammar, which marks an epoch in Hebrew learning. At the age of fourteen (1511) he took the degree of Bachelor of Arts ; three years later (1514) that of Master of Arts. In 1516 the famous Erasmus, the prince of classical scholars, gave him the testimony : " My God ! what expectations does Philip Melanchthon excite, who is yet a youth—yea, we may say a mere boy, and has already attained to equal eminence in the Greek and Latin literature ! What acumen in demonstration ! What purity and elegance of style ! What rare learning ! What comprehensive reading ! What tenderness and refinement in his extraordinary genius !" *

MELANCHTHON IN TÜBINGEN.

Melanchthon commenced his public life in the University of Tübingen, on the beautiful banks of the Neckar, as lecturer on ancient literature, and editor and commentator of Aristotle and other classics. In 1518 he

---

* *Annotat. ad Nov. Test.*, Basel, 1516, fol. 555.

published a Greek Grammar, which passed through many editions, and was used as a text-book long after his death.

The influence of his fatherly friend Reuchlin, who defended the cause of liberal learning and progress against obscurantism and stagnation, and especially the careful study of the Bible, which he carried with him everywhere, opened his eyes to the sad condition of the Church and the priesthood, and disposed him favorably to the reform movement, which commenced, during his residence at Tübingen, with the famous controversy of Luther and Tetzel (1517), and at once attracted the attention of every educated man. The protest against the profane traffic in indulgences was the occasion of the Reformation, but the cause lay deeper, in the aspirations after freedom from the fetters of popery. So the firing at Fort Sumter in South Carolina occasioned the civil war in America, while the real cause was the institution of slavery. The Ninety-five Theses of the lonely monk at Wittenberg were the spark that kindled a fire all over Europe and opened a new chapter in the history of the world.

MELANCHTHON IN WITTENBERG.

At the recommendation of Reuchlin, the Elector Frederic the Wise, of Saxony, the cautious and faithful patron of Luther, called the promising scholar from Tübingen to the Greek professorship in the University of Wittenberg, which that prince had founded in 1502, and which had just acquired a European celebrity by the outbreak of the Reformation.

Melanchthon declined calls to Ingolstadt and Leipzig, but accepted that to Wittenberg. He arrived there on the 25th of August, 1518, nearly one year after the publication of Luther's *Theses* (October 31st, 1517), and two years before the burning of the Pope's bull of excommunication (December 10th, 1520). Next to the "Luther-haus" and the Castle Church, the most interesting building in the quaint old town of Wittenberg on the banks of the Elbe is the house of Melanchthon in the Collegienstrasse. It bears the inscription on the outer wall :

> "Hier wohnte lehrte
> und starb Philipp
> Melanchthon."
> ("Here dwelt, taught, and died Philipp Melanchthon.")

It is a three-story building, and belongs to the Prussian government, King Friedrich Wilhelm IV. having bought it from its former owner. Melanchthon's study is on the first story ; there he died. Behind the house is a little garden which was connected with Luther's garden. Here, under the shade of the tree, the two Reformers may often have exchanged views on the stirring events of the times, and encouraged each other in the great conflict with popery.

Although yet a youth of twenty-one years of age, Melanchthon at once gained the esteem and admiration of his colleagues and hearers. He was small of stature, unprepossessing in his outward appearance, and extremely diffident and timid. But his high and noble forehead and his fine blue eyes, full of fire, revealed the beauty and strength of his inner man. His learning was undoubted, and his moral and religious character above suspicion. His introductory address, delivered four days after his arrival, on "the Improvement of the Studies of Youth," * dispelled all fears ; it contained the program of his academic teaching, and marks an epoch in

---

* *De Corrigendis Adolescentium Studiis*, in the *Corpus Reformatorum*, XI. 15 sqq. See Schmidt, *l. c.* 29 sq.

the history of liberal education in Germany. He desired to lead the student to the sources of knowledge, and by a careful study of the languages to furnish the key for the proper understanding of Christianity, that they might become living members of Christ and enjoy the fruits of His heavenly wisdom.

He at first devoted himself to philological pursuits, and did more than any of his contemporaries, not excepting Erasmus, to revive the study of the Greek language and literature, which did such essential service to the cause of Biblical learning, and materially promoted the triumph of the Reformation. He called the ancient languages the swaddling-clothes of the Christ-child ; Luther compared them to the sheath of the sword of the Spirit. Melanchthon was master of the ancient languages, Luther master of the German ; the former, by his co-operation, secured accuracy to the German Bible ; the latter, idiomatic force and poetic beauty.

In the year 1519 Melanchthon graduated as Bachelor of Divinity ; the degree of Doctor he modestly declined. From that time on he was a member of the theological faculty, and delivered also theological lectures, especially on exegesis. He taught two hours every day a variety of topics, including ethics, logic, Greek grammar, and literature. In the latter period of his life he devoted himself exclusively to sacred learning. He was never ordained, and never ascended the pulpit ; but for the benefit of foreign students who were ignorant of German, he delivered every Sunday in his lecture-room a Latin sermon on the Scripture lessons. He was the most popular teacher at Wittenberg.

His and Luther's fame attracted students from all parts of Christendom. He had, at times, as many as from fifteen hundred to two thousand hearers (the whole University numbered at one time three thousand students), including princes, counts, and barons, and heard occasionally as many as eleven languages at his frugal but hospitable table. Subsequently he received several calls to Tübingen, Nürnberg, and Heidelberg, and was also invited to Denmark, France, and England ; but he preferred remaining in Wittenberg till his death.

He drew up the statutes of the University, which are regarded as a model. By his advice and example the higher education in Germany was regulated.

LUTHER AND MELANCHTHON.

Immediately after his arrival at the Saxon University, on the Elbe, Melanchthon entered into an intimate relation with Luther, and became his most useful and influential co-laborer in the work of reformation. He looked up to his elder colleague with the veneration of a son, and was carried away and controlled (sometimes against his better judgment) by the fiery genius of the Protestant Elijah ; while Luther regarded him as his superior in learning and moderation, and was not ashamed to sit humbly at the feet of the modest and diffident youth. He attended several of his exegetical lectures, and published them, without his wish and knowledge, for the benefit of the Church.

The friendship of these two great men is one of the most delightful chapters in the religious drama of the sixteenth century. It rested on mutual personal esteem and hearty German affection, but especially on the consciousness of a providential mission intrusted to their united labors. Although somewhat disturbed, at a later period, by slight doctrinal differences and occasional ill-humor, it lasted to the end ; and as they worked together for the same cause, so they now rest under the same roof in the church at Wittenberg, at whose doors Luther had nailed the war-cry of the Reformation.

Melanchthon descended from South Germany, Luther from North Germany ; Melanchthon from the well-to-do middle classes of citizens and artisans, Luther from the peasantry. Melanchthon had a quiet, literary preparation for his work ; Luther experienced much hardship and severe moral conflicts. The former passed through the door of classical studies, the latter through the door of mystic contemplation and monastic asceticism ; the one was foreordained to a professor's chair, the other to the leadership of an army of conquest.

Luther best understood and expressed the difference of character, and it is one of his noble traits that he did not allow it to interfere with the esteem and admiration for his younger friend and co-worker. " I prefer the books of Master Philippus to my own," he wrote in 1529. " I am rough, boisterous, stormy, and altogether warlike, fighting against innumerable monsters and devils. I am born for the work of removing stumps and stones, cutting away thistles and thorns, and clearing the wild forests ; but Master Philippus comes along softly and gently, sowing and watering with joy, according to the gifts which God has abundantly bestowed upon him."

Luther was incomparably the stronger man of the two, and differed from Melanchthon as the wild mountain torrent differs from the quiet stream of the meadow, or as the rushing tempest from the gentle breeze, or, to use a Scriptural illustration, as the fiery Paul from the contemplative John. Luther was a man of war, Melanchthon a man of peace. Luther's writings smell of powder ; his words are battles ; he overwhelms his opponents with a roaring cannonade of argument, eloquence, passion, and abuse. Melanchthon excels in moderation and amiability, and often exercised a happy restraint upon the unmeasured violence of his colleague. Luther was a creative genius and pioneer of new paths ; Melanchthon a highly gifted scholar of untiring industry. The one was emphatically the man for the people, abounding in strong and clear sense, popular eloquence, natural wit, genial humor, intrepid courage, and straightforward honesty. The other was a quiet, considerate scholar—a man of order, method, and taste, and gained the literary circles for the cause of the Reformation. He is the principal founder of a Protestant theology. He very properly represented the evangelical cause in all the theological conferences with the Roman Catholic party at Augsburg, Speier, Worms, Frankfort, Ratisbon, where Luther's presence would only have increased the heat of controversy, and widened the breach.

Without Luther the Reformation would never have taken hold of the common people ; without Melanchthon it would never have succeeded among the scholars of Germany. The former was unyielding and uncompromising against Romanism and Zwinglianism ; the other was always ready for compromise and peace, as far as his honest convictions would allow, and sincerely labored to restore the broken unity of the Church. He was even willing, as his qualified subscription to the Articles of Smalcald shows, to admit a certain supremacy of the Pope (*jure humano*), provided he would tolerate the free preaching of the gospel. But Popery and evangelical freedom will never agree.

The one was the boldest, the most heroic and commanding ; the other, the most gentle, pious, and conscientious of the Reformers. Melanchthon had less courage, and felt, more keenly and painfully than any other,

the tremendous responsibility of the great religious movement in which he was engaged. He would have made any
personal sacrifice if he could have removed the confusion
and divisions attendant upon it.*   On several occasions
he showed, no doubt, too much timidity and weakness ;
but his concessions to the enemy, and his disposition to
compromise for peace and unity's sake, proceeded always from pure and conscientious motives.

The two Wittenberg Reformers were evidently brought
together by the hand of Providence, to supply and complete each other, and by their united talents and energies to carry forward the German Reformation, which
would have assumed a very different character if it had
been exclusively left in the hands of either of them.
Without Luther, Melanchthon would have become a
second Erasmus, though with a profounder interest in
religion, and the Reformation would have resulted in a
liberal theological school instead of giving birth to a
Church.   However much the humble and unostentatious
labors and merits of Melanchthon are overshadowed by
the more striking and brilliant deeds of the heroic
Luther, they were, in their own way, quite as useful and
indispensable.   The " still small voice " often made
friends to Protestantism where the earthquake and
thunder-storm produced only terror and convulsion.

DOMESTIC AND PRIVATE LIFE.

Melanchthon, being not an ordained clergyman or
monk, like Luther and other Reformers, had no vow of
celibacy that might hinder him from entering the mar-

---

* "*Der Schmerz der Kirchenspaltung ist tief durch seine schuldlose Seele
gegangen.*" Hase, *Kirchengesch.*, 10th ed. (1877), p. 385.

ried state. In August, 1520, when twenty-three years of age, he married Catharina Krapp, the worthy daughter of the burgomaster of Wittenberg. He followed in this step not so much his own inclination as the advice of Luther, who was anxious for his health, and hoped that a good wife would keep him from excess of study, and prolong his usefulness. Luther himself married four years later, not so much from inclination as for the purpose, as he said, of pleasing his father, teasing the pope, and vexing the devil.

Melanchthon's marriage proved a happy one, but was not free from the usual cares and trials. He declared that his wife was worthy of a better husband. His intimate friend and biographer, Camerarius, gives her a most favorable testimony. She died during his absence in Worms, in 1537. When he heard the sad news he looked up to heaven with a sigh and said, "Soon I shall follow thee." By her he had two sons and two daughters. He was a very affectionate father. Occasionally strangers would find him in the nursery, rocking the cradle with one hand and holding a book in the other. He called his house "a little church" (*ecclesiola*). He was in the habit of repeating the Apostles' Creed three times every day in his family.

His son Philip studied law, grieved his father by a secret marriage, became a notary public, and died in his eightieth year, without children. His daughter Anna married Georg Sabinus, a poet of light character, brought up in his family. She died young, and left three daughters to cheer the old age of their grandfather. His younger daughter, Magdalena, was the wife of a distinguished physician and professor, Caspar Peucer, who, after his death, ruled the University of Wittenberg, but was cruelly persecuted and kept ten years in prison by the Elector Augustus, on account of Krypto-Calvinism, of which he was the leader.

His mode of living was very simple, but free from ascetic austerity. Wittenberg was then a town of miserable dwellings in a sandy plain on the borders of civilization. Coming from the fertile Palatinate, Melanchthon complained at first that he could hardly get decent food. His highest salary was only three hundred guilders. In the first year he could not afford to buy a new dress for his wife. When Cardinal Bembo of Rome heard of his scanty support, he exclaimed : " O ungrateful Germany !" It seems that neither he nor Luther received any compensation for their books, except indirectly in the shape of occasional presents. But his hospitality and benevolence were unbounded and often abused. In this respect he was like Luther. Both had the German faculty of being happy on a small capital. They preferred plain living with high thinking to plain thinking with high living. Poverty with contentment is the lot of scholars who accomplish most for the good of the world. The apostles and ancient fathers fared no better.

Melanchthon's heart was open to tender and affectionate friendship. With Joachim Camerarius he was one heart and one soul. His relation to Luther was disturbed on the surface, but not at the bottom, and in the funeral oration he called him the Elijah who had roused the Church of God. His honesty, integrity, unselfishness, conscientiousness, and amiability are acknowledged by all. On the other hand, he was irritable, timid, and wanting in firmness of character. He unfortunately yielded his consent to the double marriage of Philip of Hesse. This is the greatest mistake which the Reformers of Germany made, and admits of no excuse. But Melanchthon repented of it so deeply that he was brought to the brink of death at Weimar in 1540.* Luther, who was made of sterner stuff, interposed for his recovery with his most earnest prayers, summoning all the resources of his faith and all the promises of God, and he succeeded.

Melanchthon's approval of the execution of Servetus for heresy is another deplorable act, but this must be charged to the intolerance of the age and the prevailing union of Church and State which made an offence against the one an offence against the other, and punishable by both. In this respect the Reformers did not rise above the theory of the Middle Ages. They had no proper conception of religious toleration and liberty.

Melanchthon shared also the traditional superstitions in regard to astrology, spectres, witchcraft, and covenants with the devil. Pope Paul III. consulted the stars before he took a journey, or convened an important consistory. Even Lord Bacon, and the great astronomers Tycho de Brahe and Kepler did not altogether reject astrology. Luther had no faith in it, and was in this respect ahead of his age. He argued against it from the example of Esau and Jacob, who were born at the same time and under the same stars, and yet of totally different character. On the other hand, Luther had personal encounters with the Evil One, and threw the inkstand at him in the Wartburg. He also believed in the motion of the sun around the earth, and objected, in a conversation with Melanchthon, to the Copernican system that Joshua bade the sun to stand still, and not the earth.

---

* " *Wie hat der Teufel dieses Organon geschändet !*" said Luther, when he saw the corpse-like form of his friend.

THE CLOSING YEARS.

After Luther's death, in 1546, Melanchthon lost the strongest outward support of his character, and his natural timidity and irresoluteness appeared more prominently than before. The times also became too violent for so peaceful a man. The war between Catholics and Protestants broke out at last. Charles V. defeated the Lutheran princes at Mühlberg (April 24th, 1547), entered Wittenberg, and stood thoughtful before the grave of Luther, in the castle church. Although he regretted that he had not burned the archheretic at Worms, he promptly declined the proposal of one of his generals, to dig up and burn his bones and to scatter the ashes to the four winds, with the noble and dignified answer : "I war against the living, not the dead." The University was dissolved. Melanchthon fled with his family and Luther's widow to Braunschweig, and afterward to Nordhausen. He returned after the victory of Elector Moritz of Saxony over the Emperor, and labored twelve more years at the head of the University, which rose again to a high degree of prosperity. He was consulted from near and far as a sort of oracle in theology and education. But he was violently assailed from Magdeburg and Jena by Flacius, his former pupil and *protégé*, by Westphal, Hesshusius, and other fanatical Lutherans, who forgot his invaluable services to the Lutheran Church, and openly charged him with treason to the cause of truth.

The ground of this charge was his yielding disposition to Popery on the one hand, and to Calvinism on the other. He submitted to the Augsburg and Leipzig compromises, called *Interim*, which the Emperor imposed upon the Protestants, but which fell to pieces with his defeat. Melanchthon had not the courage of a martyr, and hoped by submission to ceremonies in themselves indifferent to prevent the reintroduction of Popery and to save the cause of the Reformation for better times. He gave still greater offence to the same bigoted party by his growing disposition to unite with the Reformed, which was strengthened by his intimate personal and theological friendship with Calvin since they met at theological conferences in 1539 and 1540. He mastered his sensitive temper, and answered the attacks of his former friends and pupils by silence. He sought to gain his enemies by kindness. The violent controversies in the Lutheran Church continued long after his death, and were adjusted at last by the "Formula of Concord" and the triumph of strict Lutheran orthodoxy (1577).

Add to these public calamities and personal attacks the growing weakness and sickness of the body, and various domestic bereavements, and we need not wonder that the last years of Melanchthon were years of grief and sorrow rather than of joy and pleasure. He experienced the full measure of that melancholy which cast its shade over the closing scenes of Luther, and many other great and good men. He often prayed to be delivered from the "fury of theologians" (*rabies theologorum*).

His personal sufferings, however, did not affect him near as much as his care for the Church. He uttered the noble sentiment : "If my eyes were a fountain of tears, as rich as the river Elbe, I could not sufficiently express my sorrow over the divisions and distractions of Christians." His heart and soul longed and prayed, in unison with the spirit of his divine Master, that all believers "may be perfected into one," even as He and the Father are one (John xvii. 23). His last lecture treated of Christ's agony in Gethsemane, his last sermon was on the sacerdotal prayer of our Lord.

HIS DEATH.

Finally, the hour of his deliverance came. He died peacefully on the 19th of April, 1560, aged sixty-three years, in the presence of about twenty friends and relatives, who were greatly edified by his prayers and patience during his last sufferings. He found much comfort in the following thoughts, which he had written down in Latin on a piece of paper : on one side, " Thou shalt be free from sin, free from cares, and from the fury of theologians ;" on the other side : " Thou shalt come into the light, thou shalt see God and behold the Son of God ; thou shalt learn those wonderful mysteries which pass our comprehension in this life, as the cause of our creation and present condition, the mystery of the union of the divine and human nature in Christ." His sole care was not for himself, but for the unity and peace of the Church. When Professor Peucer, his son-in-law, asked him, a few hours before his departure, whether he desired anything, he answered : " Nothing but heaven."

His last audible words were a hearty yea and amen to the prayer of the Psalmist (Ps. xxxi. 5), recited by one of his colleagues : " Into Thine hand I commend my spirit : Thou hast redeemed me, O Lord, Thou God of truth !"

During the polemical era of the seventeenth century Melanchthon's name was under a cloud. But with the revival of evangelical theology in the nineteenth century his memory was revived. On April 9th, 1860, the tricentennial celebration of his death was held with great enthusiasm throughout Protestant Germany. At Wittenberg, where " he lived, taught, and died " (as the inscription on his house reads), the corner-stone of a noble monument to his memory, erected at the side of that of Luther, was laid on that occasion in the name of the King of Prussia, by his brother, the Prince Regent, now Emperor of Germany. The festival oration was delivered by the venerable Dr. Nitzsch, of Berlin, the last surviving professor of the once famous University of Wittenberg, now merged in that of Halle. There is now no Protestant divine of any weight in Europe or America who does not pronounce the name of Melanchthon with veneration and gratitude.

HIS PUBLIC CHARACTER AND SERVICES.

Melanchthon is the model of a Christian scholar. He combined the highest scientific and literary culture which was attainable in his age, with an humble and childlike Christian faith. Love to God and to man and supreme regard to truth animated and controlled his studies and whole life.

He was emphatically the theologian of the Lutheran Church, and posterity gave him the honorable title " *Præceptor Germaniæ.* " He was a man of thought, not of action. Luther was great in both, and in this resembled St. Paul. Luther produced ideas, and expressed them very clearly, with original force and freshness, but not in logical, systematic form, and often with too great polemical vehemence, and regardless of their connections and consequences. He did not fear to contradict himself, and always spoke as he felt at the moment. Melanchthon's mind, though far less vigorous and original, was much better disciplined and proportioned, more calm and circumspect.

The literary fertility of Melanchthon is astounding. His works fill twenty-eight large volumes of the *Cor-*

pus Reformatorum, edited by Bretschneider and Bind-
seil (1836-60). They embrace theology, philosophy,
philology, methodology, and the science of education.
He wrote a large number of manuals, dissertations, ora-
tions, polemical tracts, church ordinances, counsels, prefaces, and letters.

His greatest work is the *Augsburg Confession*, the
most important and most generally received creed of the
Lutheran Church. He drew it up, during the German
Diet of 1530, with the utmost care, moderation, and conscientiousness ; and he afterward, though without authority, improved and altered it in the edition of 1540, to
make it acceptable to the Reformed. Hence the distinction between the " altered " and " unaltered " Confession of Augsburg. The former has often been sub-
scribed by German Reformed Churches ; also by Calvin,
while at Strassburg ; but it was disowned by orthodox
Lutherans, and gave rise to violent disputes. He also wrote
the *Apology of the Augsburg Confession*, in opposition to
the Roman *Refutation ;* and it likewise gradually assumed symbolical authority in the Lutheran Church. It is
one of the best theological treatises of that excited period.

He issued the first Protestant system of didactic theology, under the title *Loci Communes Rerum Theolo-
gicarum* (first edition, December, 1521). They proceeded from his lectures on the Epistle to the Romans.
Although very defective in the first editions, and afterward surpassed by Calvin's *Institutes*, the book is remarkable for its simplicity, clearness, freshness, and
thoroughly evangelical tone. Luther thought it worthy
of a place in the canon.* It passed through five revis-

---

* He called it " *liber invictus, non solum immortalitate, sed et canone
ecclesiastico dignus.*"

ions and more than thirty editions before the author's
death, and was used, long afterward, as a text-book of
didactic theology in the Lutheran universities, as the
"Sentences" of Peter the Lombard had been used, for
the same purpose, in the Middle Ages.   Strange that
the two greatest dogmatic works of the Reformation
were produced by lay theologians ; for neither Melanchthon nor Calvin were ordained by human hands, but
both fully made good the evangelical principle of the
general priesthood of believers.

Besides, we have from Melanchthon a number of
Biblical Commentaries.   They are not near as satisfactory as one might expect from his superior classical
attainments, and were far surpassed by those of Luther,
Calvin, and Beza ; yet they were extremely popular
with the hearers, and served a valuable purpose in bringing to light the natural sense, and evangelical ideas of the
Scriptures in support of the cause of the Reformation.

Melanchthon's theology was not so consistent throughout as that of Calvin, who had a more philosophical and
logical mind, and rose at a more advanced period of the
Reformation.   His changes may be regarded as an evidence of a want of independence and stability ; but they
prove also the flexible and progressive character of his
mind, and his willingness to learn and improve, even
in old age, and honestly to retract his errors.   They
grew, moreover, out of the nature of the Protestant
movement, in its first stages, which was not the result of
a previous calculation, but a gradual historical process.
Like Luther, Melanchthon developed his system before
the eyes of the public, keeping pace with the progress of the Reformation itself.   The overbearing influence of Luther, too, carried him unconsciously to many
extreme positions, which on calmer reflection, especially

after Luther's death, he felt it his duty to modify. While Luther held fast to the views he once had acquired, Melanchthon subjected his views to constant revision with his expanding knowledge. His theology was in perpetual motion, but his fundamental religious convictions and his love to Christ remained unchanged and deepened under all his theological changes.

Thus he gave up the rigid view of an absolute predestination of good and evil, which he had expressed in the first edition of his *Loci Theologici*, and in his Commentary on the Epistle to the Romans (1523), in almost as strong terms as Luther had done in his tract on " The Slavery of the Human Will," against Erasmus (1525). He traced the adultery of David and the treason of Judas, as well as the conversion of Paul, to a divine decree. But in the later editions of his *Loci* he adopted what has been termed the *synergistic* scheme : teaching a co-operation of the preceding divine and the consenting human will in the work of conversion and sanctification, and throwing the responsibility of perdition upon the disobedient will of the sinner. He anticipated in part the Arminian theory, which half a century after his death sprung up in Holland. He also modified the doctrine of justification by faith alone, so as to lay greater stress upon the necessity for good works than he or Luther had done before—not, indeed, as a cause, but as an indispensable evidence of justification.

These changes in the articles of predestination, freedom, and justification may be regarded in the light of a concession and approach to the Catholic system, without giving up, however, the essentially evangelical basis.

On the other hand, in the sacramental controversy, he evidently made an approach, since 1534, and more decidedly in 1540 (when he changed the tenth article of

the Augsburg Confession), to the Reformed type of doctrine, by relaxing the Lutheran theory of the real cor-
poreal presence of Christ in, with, and under the elements
of the Eucharist, and leaning to Calvin's view of a
spiritual real presence and fruition of Christ's body and
blood, by faith.   For reasons of prudence and from love
of peace he declined, in his old age, to take an active
part in the renewed sacramental war between Westphal
and Calvin, and to a give a final, unmistakable expression of his views on this mysterious subject.   He hoped
that both theories might be tolerated in the evangelical
churches.   One of his last acts and testimonies, in the
very year of his death, was a protest against the exclu-
siveness of the bigoted Hesshusins, and a virtual indorse-
ment of the position of the Reformed party at Heidelberg, which immediately afterward triumphed in the
Palatinate, under the lead of his favorite pupil, Zacharias
Ursinus, the Calvinist Caspar Olevianus, and the pious
Elector Frederic III.   His mild, amiable, and peaceful
spirit breathes in the Heidelberg Catechism, which was
prepared by these divines by order of the Elector and
became the doctrinal standard of the German and Dutch
Reformed Churches in Europe and America.

Melanchthon thus is a connecting link between the
Lutheran and Reformed Confessions, equally honored by
both.   He represents the spirit and aim of Christian
union on the basis of the everlasting gospel as revealed
in the New Testament and in the life and example of
our Lord.   To him applies the beatitude :

"Blessed are the peacemakers : for they shall be
called the children of God."

REMINISCENCES OF NEANDER.

THE life of Neander, "the Father of Church History," was spent in the study and lecture-room, among books and with students, but is not without romantic interest, especially his youth. He had a strongly marked individuality above most of his contemporaries, and passed through striking changes in his religious experience.

---

[*] A biography of Neander, though long expected, is still a desideratum. The task was intrusted to his pupil, Dr. Schneider, but he never found leisure to carry it out. We have, however, important contributions, viz., Neander's Letters to the poet Chamisso (in Chamisso's works) from the period of his youth, and his paper which contains a sort of baptismal confession (1805, first published by Kling, 1851); Krabbe's *Charakteristik Neander's* (Hamburg, 1852); Hagenbach's article on Neander's *Verdienste um die Kirchengeschichte* (in the *Studien und Kritiken*, 1851); Ullmann's admirable Preface to the third edition of Neander's *Kirchengeschichte* (translated in the first vol. of the Am. ed.); Professor Jacobi's *Erinnerungen an Neander* (from one of his faithful pupils, Halle, 1882); and Uhlhorn's article in Herzog's *Encyklopædie*, revised ed., vol. x., 447–457 (abridged in Schaff-Herzog, II., p. 1612 sqq.). The author of these *Reminiscences* wrote several brief sketches of Neander, in his *Kirchenfreund* (1851); in *Germany, its Universities and Divines* (Philadelphia, 1857), in Appletons' *Am. Cyclopædia*, and in Funk's *Homiletic Review* (New York, 1885); but this is fuller than any. The first centennial of Neander's birth will no doubt be celebrated in 1889, as the centennial of Schleiermacher's birth was celebrated in 1868. Then we may expect a number of commemorative addresses, and perhaps a full biography worthy of his name.

His original name was *David Mendel*. He was born of Jewish parents, at Göttingen, on January 17th, 1789 (the year of the French Revolution), converted to Christianity, and baptized at Hamburg, under the significant name of *Neander* (νέος ἀνήρ, *New-man*), in his seventeenth year, on February 15th, 1806.

He received his classical education in the Gymnasium (Johanneum) at Hamburg (1803–1806), under the direction of the learned John Gurlitt. He at once attracted the attention of teachers and students by the contrast between his appearance and attainments. He had hardly body enough to shelter his mind. He looked like a simpleton, and yet took the lead of his class in industry and progress. His memory was extraordinary, and he soon became as familiar with Latin and Greek as with his native tongue. The thoughtless indulged in sports at his expense, but he ignored them, and lived in a world of abstraction. It is related of Thomas Aquinas, the master theologian of the Middle Ages, that he was despised by his fellow-students and called *bos mutus;* but after he opened his mouth in an academic disputation, his teacher, Albertus Magnus, exclaimed : " We call him the *mute ox*, but his voice will soon be heard throughout the world !" And the prophecy was fulfilled.

Neander stood a brilliant examination when he left college, and delivered, April 30th, 1805, with clear, sonorous voice, a parting address, *De Judæis optima conditione in civitatem recipiendis.* He then entered the academic department of the Johanneum, to prepare more thoroughly for the University. His mother wished him to become a merchant. for which calling, although a Jew, he was absolutely unfit. He himself first intended to study law, like Luther and Calvin, but soon wisely exchanged it for theology, and stuck to it. Being very

I

poor, he was supported by Dr. Stieglitz and a scholarship which Gurlitt secured for him.

From 1806 to 1809 he pursued his studies in the Universities of Halle and Göttingen. In Halle the mighty genius of Schleiermacher introduced him into the principles of Christian dogmatics and ethics; but the suspension of the University by Napoleon, after the battle of Jena, compelled him to flee. He travelled with Neumann on foot to Göttingen, where he arrived fatigued and pennyless, but was kindly received by Gesenius, the eminent Hebrew scholar. He attended chiefly the lectures of Planck, the pragmatic historian of the doctrinal controversies in the Lutheran Church, to whom he afterward dedicated, with filial gratitude, a volume of his *Church History.* He was urged by him to remain in Göttingen as *Repetent,* and to devote himself to the academic career.

But Neander returned to Hamburg, and was examined for the ministry. He preached his first sermon at Wandsbeck, near Hamburg, on the Divine Logos (John 1 : 1); but he was evidently better fitted for the chair than the pulpit. At one time his manuscript flew down upon his hearers, but he preached on as if nothing had happened. His favorite study was now the Gospel of John. His friendship with Claudius of Wandsbeck led him more deeply into practical Christianity. In 1810 he made the acquaintance of the Swabian poets Karl Mayer, Gustav Schwab, and Justinus Kerner.

In the autumn of 1810 he went to Heidelberg, and his mother and sisters soon followed him, to take care of his feeble health. In the following year he began his academic career as *Privatdocent* of Theology in that University, on the banks of the Neckar, with a dissertation on the relation between knowledge and faith, as conceived by Clement of Alexandria. In 1812 he was already made Professor Extraordinary, and published a monograph on Julian the Apostate. This book settled at once his vocation as an historian of the Christian religion.

In 1813, yet a youth like Melanchthon, whom he strongly resembles in other respects also, he received, at Schleiermacher's suggestion, a call as Professor of Church History in the University of Berlin, which had been founded a few years before (1810). This youngest of the German Universities rose with unexampled rapidity to the first rank through the fame of eminent teachers in every branch of science and literature, such as Schleiermacher, Neander, Marheincke, De Wette, Tholuck, Hengstenberg, in theology; Fichte, Hegel, Schelling, in philosophy; Böckh, and Lachmann, in classical philology; Savigny, and Stahl, in jurisprudence; Ritter, in geography; Ranke, in history, the last survivor of that wonderful galaxy.

Neander labored in Berlin as lecturer and writer, by doctrine and by example, incessantly till his death, on the 14th of July, 1850. Only now and then he broke the uniformity of his existence by a vacation trip, in company with his sister or with some student, for the benefit of his feeble health, and to consult rare books and unpublished manuscripts in the libraries at Vienna, Munich, and other cities. On these journeys he usually had with him a trunk full of church fathers, "for a little reading on the way." He led the life of a learned Benedictine in the midst of a noisy city. He had always a crowded lecture-room, and was the most popular and useful, as well as the most esteemed and beloved professor of that great University during its first half century. His chair has never as yet been filled by a successor of equal power and influence.

NEANDER'S TRAINING FOR HIS WORK.

Behind the simple framework of his outer existence lay hid a rich intellectual and spiritual life. It is interesting to follow its gradual development on to full maturity, and to trace the different influences which led him to his peculiar theological standpoint and his calling as an historian of Christianity.

Among these influences we must first mention his descent from that wonderful people which was intrusted with the oldest revelations of God, and which, like the bush of Horeb, shines and burns in history without being consumed. His father was a common Jewish peddler and usurer, and neglected to provide for his family. But his mother, Esther (*née* Gottschalk), was a respectable, pious, and agreeable Jewess, and related to the philosopher, Moses Mendelssohn, of Berlin, and the Medical Counsellor, Dr. Stieglitz, of Hanover. Soon after the birth of David, her youngest child, she separated from her worthless husband, removed with her five children to Hamburg, and struggled hard to support them. Neander cherished her memory, and no doubt thought of her when he described the moulding influence of pious mothers upon the ancient fathers. He ever regarded Hamburg as his proper home, and gave it a substantial proof of affection at the great fire of 1842, by a liberal contribution of one thousand Prussian dollars for the relief of the sufferers. Göttingen, his real birthplace, he called "Philistropolis." His brothers and sisters, and finally also his mother, left the synagogue and embraced the Christian religion. His sister Hannah accompanied him as a guardian angel through life.*

---

* His oldest brother, Dr. Andr. K. Joh. Mendel, born 1780, an

If there ever was a sincere and intelligent convert from Judaism to Christianity it is Neander. The new name which he assumed at his baptism in 1806, was JOHANN AUGUST WILHELM NEANDER, in memory of *Johann* Gurlitt, his teacher, *August* Varnhagen von Ense, and *Wilhelm Neumann*, his friends who assisted as sponsors. His chief name expressed at the same time the fact that he had become a new creature in Christ Jesus. He belongs to the line of converts which begins with Paul of Tarsus. His transition was less abrupt and radical than that of the former persecutor, but he resembles the Apostle of the Gentiles in purity of motive, strength of conviction, unselfish devotion to the religion of his choice, and zeal for the freedom in Christ from the bondage of legalism, as also in the weakness (if not the awkwardness) of his " bodily presence" (2 Cor. 10 : 10). He bore the heavenly treasure in an earthen vessel. When the King of Prussia once asked him, " What is the best evidence of Christianity?" he is said to have replied, " The Jews, your Majesty."

The second controlling element in his training was the philosophy of Plato, which of all heathen philosophies approaches nearest to the gospel, and aided in the conversion of Justin Martyr, Augustin, and other ancient

---

esteemed physician, was baptized June 25th, 1806, and died, unmarried, of typhoid fever. His second brother, a travelling merchant, had been baptized two years before Neander, and died insane, as also his sister Betty. The oldest sister, Henriette Scholz, born 1777, embraced Christianity in 1807. His second sister, Hannchen, born 1782, was baptized on March 22d, 1807. The youngest sister, Betty, born 1788, became a Christian on November 7th, 1809, and finally the mother professed the same faith in 1810, shortly before Neander's removal to Heidelberg. See Kling, in Ullmann's " Studien und Kritiken," 1851, p. 516 sqq. I knew personally Mrs. Scholz and her daughter, and Hannchen Neander.

fathers. It fulfilled a similar office in Neander. It kindled in him an enthusiasm for the ideals of truth, beauty, and goodness. William Neumann, his fellow-student in the academic college at Hamburg, wrote of him, February 11th, 1806 : " Plato is his idol and never-ceasing war-cry. He sits day and night over him, and there are few who received him so fully and with such purity of soul. Upon the world round about he looks with supreme contempt." Next to the Dialogues of Plato he admired and studied the moral treatises and biographies of the noble Plutarch. He joined with sympathizing friends a philosophico-poetical society under the name of the " Polar Star" (τὸ τοῦ πόλου ἄστρον), and explained in the evening meetings Plato and Sophocles.

He was also, like Schleiermacher, in early contact with the Romantic school of the two brothers Schlegel, Tieck, and Novalis, which revived the poetry and religion of the Middle Ages in opposition to the cold and dreary scepticism of the times.

But the Platonic idealism and Romantic sentimental-ism could not satisfy his mind. He found rest in a solid Christian realism.

Last, though not least, we must mention the stimulat-ing influence of Schleiermacher, the German Plato, who, by his *Discourses on Religion* (1799), like a priest in the outer court of nature, conducted so many of the noblest and most gifted youths of Germany out of the dry heath of the then dominant Rationalism to the garden of Revelation. Neander read his *Discourses*, and *Mono-logues* with enthusiasm, before he heard his lectures at Halle. He stood indebted to him, as he himself cheer-fully acknowledged, for manifold quickening impulses, and they remained good friends as colleagues through life, although they differed in weighty points. Neander had a much stronger sense of sin, and no sympathy with pantheism, and was more positive and realistic in his religious convictions. He was inferior to Schleiermacher as an original thinker and system-builder, but surpassed him as a regenerator of practical religion among the students of Germany. Schleiermacher was admired and feared ; Neander was esteemed and beloved. Schleiermacher stimulated the intellect ; Neander moved the heart. He announced to his students the death of Schleiermacher, February 12th, 1834, with these words : "To-day the man passed away from whom in future a new epoch in theology will be dated." They remind one of the way in which Melanchthon announced in the lecture-room the death of Luther.

The fermentation produced in his mind by these various influences is reflected in an unripe but very remarkable essay from his pen, which he addressed to a pastor in Hamburg before his baptism, and which was first published after his death by Dr. Kling in 1851.* It is an attempt to trace the epochs in the development of religion, and strangely mixes Platonism, Romanticism, and Christianity, but arrives at the satisfactory conclusion : "I recognize in the Christian religion the absolute truth, the most perfect religion, the only way to salvation." He passed, as it were, before his conversion,

---

* In Ullmann's *Studien und Kritiken*, 1851, No. II., p. 460 sqq. ; and in Schaff's *Deutsche Kirchenfreund* for 1851, p. 283–297. The manuscript bears the title : "*Ein Versuch, die Religion in ihren Entwicklungsstufen dialektisch zu construiren*," with the marginal note of Pastor Bossau . "*Von A. Neander, als er 16 Jahre alt war.*" It was handed to Bossau by Neander, and then came into the possession of P. Baring, Bossau's son-in-law, who lent it to Dr. Kling for publication.

through the world-historical process of preparation for the advent of the Saviour of mankind.

Thus was Neander fitted out for his life-work, to be the historian of Christianity. Moses and Plato were the tutors who led him to Christ and enabled him to view the Christian religion as the fulfilment of all the nobler aspirations of the Jewish and Gentile world, and as the final and perfect religion of mankind. Before him church history had been degraded by German Rationalism into a godless history of human errors and follies. Neander effected a revolution. He revealed in it a golden chain of manifestations of Christ's truth and love and a fulfilment of His promise to be with His disciples to the end of the world. He showed it to be a continuous commentary on the parable of the leaven which gradually leavens the whole lump of humanity. He traced the footsteps of the Redeemer in all His followers. He sympathized with everything that is Christian, whether he found it in the Greek or Roman or Evangelical churches, or among persecuted heretics. He had no sectarian or partisan zeal. He viewed and judged all phenomena from the Christological centre. Truth and justice were his sole aim. His charity was as broad as humanity. He thus made church history a book of instruction, edification, and comfort, on the firm foundation of profound and accurate learning, critical mastery of the sources, spiritual discernment, psychological insight, and sound, sober judgment. In the hands of Rationalists and Deists church history was a dreary desert. Neander changed it into a garden of God, full of flowers and fruits.

In his large-hearted Christian sympathy and catholicity lies his chief and lasting merit as an historian. It makes him a blessing to all denominations. The earlier vol-

umes of his *History* have been superseded in part by the
rapid progress of discovery and research since his death,
but they will nevertheless continue to be a mine of intellectual and spiritual wealth ; while the spirit of evangelical catholicity which pervades all his works is a perma-
nent gain and a wholesome stimulus and guide to every
student of theology.

But we do not intend here to enlarge on his writings,
of which we have spoken elsewhere. We confine ourselves to personal reminiscences of what he was as a man,
as a teacher, and as a Christian.

THE OUTWARD APPEARANCE.

In his appearance, to begin with what struck every one
in an unusual degree, Neander was a perfect original—
we might say, one of the rarest natural curiosities. Yet
his uncommon exterior betokened an uncommon interior.
Even his clothing—a well-worn coat of ancient cut (we
never knew him to wear a dress-coat) ; jack-boots reaching above the knees ; a white cravat carelessly tied,
often on one side of the neck, or behind it ; an old-fashioned hat set aslant on the back of his head—all this
presented an oddity which seemed to mock the elegant
refinement of Berlin, and yet he was greeted respectfully
by everybody who knew him, from the king to the
lounger at the street-corner.

He was of a slender bodily frame, of middling size,
with strongly marked Jewish, though at the same time
most benevolent and good-natured, features ; the eyes,
deeply seated and full of fire, were overshadowed, as
with an umbrella, by an unusually strong, bushy pair of
eyebrows.

Thus he sat in his solitary study in the Markgrafen
Strasse, No. 51, surrounded with the spirits of church

fathers, schoolmen, mystics, and reformers, whose works lay on all sides in learned disorder—against the walls, on the floor, on tables and chairs—so that visitors could scarcely find a place on an old-fashioned sofa for sitting down ; while the way out into the dining-room and into the decently furnished parlor of his sister led over the printed monuments of bygone ages.

His absolute freedom from all that belongs to the show of vanity, and his indifference to things external, gave occasion to ludicrous anecdotes. He walked once through the streets with a broom under his arm instead of an umbrella. Another time, in the lecture-room, he took a brush out of his pocket instead of his note-book. Being lost in the streets, he called to a cabman to take him home, and was surprised that he did not know the number of the house, saying, " My good man, I thought you knew it, as you are a droschky driver." They waited till a student accidentally arrived and relieved them of embarrassment. When the tailor brought him a new pair of pantaloons, he put them on over the old the wrong way, and cut off one leg as superfluous. Once he set off for the university in his dressing-gown, but was happily fetched back by his amanuensis. On another occasion, having once got with one foot into the gutter, he hobbled along the whole length of the street in this predicament ; and as soon as he reached home, he sent for a physician to cure him of his imaginary lameness. *Se non e vero, e ben trovato.* I cannot vouch for these funny stories ; some, no doubt, had their origin in the creative imagination of his students, or were exaggerations of facts. But it is quite certain that the German professor had less common than uncommon sense, and moved in an ideal world, with his eyes half shut to the real world around him.

NEANDER IN THE LECTURE-ROOM.

Still more odd, if possible, was the appearance of the good man on the rostrum.* As he could hardly have found the way by himself, and must have been put in danger by the moving crowd of vehicles and men, a student accompanied him from the Markgrafen Strasse, passing the royal library and the Opera-platz to the university building unter den Linden. From the reading-room, where the professors meet during recess, he proceeded alone into his lecture-room, which was quite close at hand, shooting in sideways ; he seized, first of all, a couple of goose-quills, which must be regularly laid upon the desk beforehand, to keep his fingers employed, and then began his lecture, without any other help than that of some illegible notes and citations. There he stood, constantly changing the position of his feet ; bent forward, frequently sinking his head, and then again throwing it on high, especially when roused to polemic zeal against pantheism or formalism—at times threatening even to overturn the rostrum—but all the while spinning forth from his mind a train of facts and ideas with intense earnestness, or unfolding, with penetrating insight and loving sympathy, the development of a Christian doctrine, or the principles of Christian ethics, or the spiritual character of a great and good man.

The whole scene was so strange and eccentric that one who heard him for the first time could hardly contain himself for astonishment, and had no power at all to follow him with the pen. And yet the earnestness and the enthusiasm of the eccentric professor, the extraordinary

---

* In my book on *German Universities* (1857) I gave a picture of Neander in the lecture-room, drawn by one of his students.

learning and profound thought that flowed in an incessant stream from his head and heart, restrained all laughter—nay, his personal aspect itself had always, even on the first acquaintance, something that inspired reverence and at the same time called forth confidence and love. In a short time, moreover, one grew accustomed to his strange exterior, the comical form vanished before its own solid contents, and served only to make him the object of higher admiration. For Neander all this was perfectly natural, without the remotest thought of effect. Altogether there never was a man more free from affectation and ostentation.

HOME LIFE.

All these singularities of his outward appearance indicated that he was a stranger on this earth, and that he was formed wholly for the kingdom of heaven. His ignorance of worldly life and business, his freedom from the temptations of vanity, his superiority to much that, for others, forms an indispensable need, his indifference toward the material side of existence, fitted him for his purely inward calling and for undisturbed communion with the quiet spirit-world of the past.

"He was," as Hase characterizes him, "a monk in his habits, poor for himself, rich for others." His wants were very few. He was as abstemious in practice as an ancient ascetic, but liberal in theory, and very hospitable. He entertained the students once a week at the tea-table, and often gave dinner-parties to friends, talking theology, while they enjoyed the dinner, and listened to his wisdom.

He was never married, and consecrated his whole time to the service of the Lord, as an eunuch for the kingdom of God's sake (Matt. xix. 12). He belonged to the exceptions, for whom the life of celibacy is a moral duty, and the means of greater activity and success, as it was for Paul and Barnabas. A lady friend once jokingly suggested a companion to him ; he looked perplexed, and asked : "How could I find time for courting ?" An American pro-slavery divine created considerable merriment at Neander's dinner-table when he asked him, whether he would be willing by marriage with a colored woman to give practical proof of his doctrine of equality, which he so emphatically asserted.

HANNAH NEANDER.

Instead of a wife, however, God had given him a true female companion in the person of an unmarried sister, who sacrificed a youthful attachment for his sake, followed him from Judaism to Christianity, assumed the care of his modest wants with the most tender devotion, attended him almost daily in his walks *unter den Linden* and in the *Thiergarten*, kept him informed about the latest German and English novels, and with kind hospitality entertained his numerous friends and pupils.

Sister Hannah, or Hannchen, was also highly peculiar : like him, intensely Jewish outside and intensely Christian inside ; highly intellectual, not wanting in genuine wit and literary culture, but at the same time a good housekeeper and altogether a very sensible, practical person, supplying thus her brother's defect. When she brought him his breakfast or a glass of water, he knew that he must be hungry or thirsty ; when she gave him medicine, he took it like a child ; when she provided for him a new suit, he put it on, unless she forgot to take away the old one.

The peaceful and innocent living together of this original pair, called the "Neander children," had in it something uncommonly touching, and no one could mistake the wise hand of Providence in their connection, for the accomplishment of the great spiritual work to which Neander had been predestinated.

Miss Hannah Neander survived her brother four years. I saw her last on a visit to Berlin, in the spring of 1854, sitting before his bust, with tears in her eyes, indulging in reminiscences of their happy life, and longing to join him in the better world. It was a most affecting interview. A few weeks afterward her mortal remains were laid beside those of her brother in the Jerusalem Cemetery of Berlin, to rest till the day of resurrection.

NEANDER AS A TEACHER.

Neander was an enthusiastic teacher. He had that rare personal magnetism which drew the hearers irresistibly into the current of his thoughts, and made them forget everything else. He prepared himself most carefully for his lectures, and threw his whole soul into them. He was *totus in illis.* He made the labors of authorship subservient to his immediate duty as professor. He gave the students the best results of his unwearied studies in ever fresh reproduction and adaptation to the times. He tried to reach their heart as well as their intellect, and first and last to lead them to Christ, as the pure source of all wisdom. His own self was absorbed in the cause. He impressed them with the conviction : here is a thoroughly learned and thoroughly good man, who speaks from the overflowing fullness of knowledge and experience, with the single purpose of promoting the glory of Christ and the good of his fellow-men. His lectures were inspiring and edifying as well as instructive.

What he said of Schelling was even more true of himself : " He awakened in the German youth that love which gives wings for soaring on high (the ἔρως πτερο-φύτωρ)." * His mission, says Ullmann, was " to light up a fire in the soul ; and hardly any other teacher has succeeded in doing it so well."

No wonder that the students were enthusiastically devoted to him in return. As often as his birthday came round they brought him some suitable present and a serenade, to which was added not unfrequently a grand torchlight procession ; not only his own immediate pupils, but students also from the other faculties, joining with lively interest in the occasion.

NEANDER AS A FRIEND OF THE STUDENTS.

His interest in the students was not confined to the lecture-room. He had toward them the feelings of a friend and a father, as well as a teacher, and they filled the place of sons who were denied him.

Never, perhaps, was the love of a professor toward his pupils so deep and strong. Tholuck alone, among contemporary divines, could compare with him in this respect : he, too, had no children, but a most excellent wife, and adopted, as it were, the students as his sons and companions on his daily promenades and in his house.

Neander used to invite as many students as his room would hold to tea on Saturday evening. He led the conversation in a low, deep voice, entered with affectionate sympathy into their thoughts and feelings, and answered their questions, while playing with a goose-quill

---

* See his dedicatory preface to Schelling of the first volume of his revised *Church History*, which appeared in 1842, after Schelling's lectures in Berlin.

or kneading a bit of wax in his fingers. He never used tobacco in any form, but such innocent occupations of the hand seemed to facilitate the movements of his mind. The venerable Nitzsch, his friend and colleague, had the habit in the lecture-room to unbutton his coat from bottom to top, then to take a pinch of snuff, and slowly to button the coat again, and to repeat this process to the end of the lecture.

While Neander presided over the theological discussions, his sister attended to the tea-table, indulged in innocent small talk, harmless jokes and merry laughs, propounded riddles, told funny anecdotes and marvellous ghost stories, or asked such embarrassing questions as, "Herr Candidat, are you engaged to be married?" Though an old-maid herself, her heart kept young and fresh, and, like her brother, she felt most at home among students. Hospitable as he was, he seldom accepted invitations, and then only for the sake of his sister.

The professors of German Universities receive a part of their income from the lecture fees of students. To get a remission of the *honorarium* from Neander was the easiest thing in the world; and he was very often imposed upon by those who might easily have paid the small sum. The Society for Sick Students in Berlin, founded by his pupils on his birthday, 1826, owed its origin to him, and he devoted to it the whole profits of some of his writings (his *Gelegenheitsschriften*, which passed through several editions), as he gave the copy money he received for other works to Bible societies. Every one in want or need found in him a sympathizing heart and liberal hand.

I have still a lively remembrance of his interest in a young man who was blind. Earnestly thirsting after religious knowledge, the youth had attended his lectures in 1840 on church history and exegesis, and spoke afterward with grateful satisfaction of the spiritual benefit they had afforded him. When Neander heard of his poverty, he showed great emotion, inquired with staring eyes and nervous agitation into all the details, and then hurried away to his sister to procure him help. I happened to be in his study at the time, and the scene struck me the more deeply, as Neander, by reason of his total lack of practical tact, had himself the air of one perfectly helpless ; and with his eager readiness to assist want, was still in a quandary as to how it should be done, till his sister or amanuensis came to his relief. And how much good did he do which never came to light ! for he was the man precisely to abhor all show, and not let his left hand know what was done by his right.

Neander gave touching expression to the tenderness of his friendship in his dedicatory prefaces, and especially in his memorial tribute to Hermann Rossel, one of his favorite and most promising students, who died in the spring of life. Another proof came to light long after his death in a letter published by a " Septuagenarian Soldier" in the *Evangelical Church Gazette* of Berlin (September, 1867). This soldier when a young man, in 1823, called on Neander, whom he knew only from his writings, for advice and comfort, being in great spiritual doubt and conflict. The professor stopped his work, encouraged the stranger, accompanied him down-stairs, and wrote to him the following effective letter of comfort :

" MY DEAR FRIEND : My thoughts have been constantly full of you and of your condition ever since I became acquainted with your warm heart, and my heartiest prayers and desires ascend to heaven that He, from whom cometh down every good gift, and who has promised to be always near to the bruised and burdened heart, will give you His peace, and that He will heal your wounded heart with

K

His own infinite love, so richly given us in Christ Jesus! This will surely be, if you only do not make yourself unhappy; instead of clinging to yourself, let your thoughts go out like a child toward Him, without whom you cannot indeed feel your misery, which we all, as poor sinners, share with you—and let yourself be led by Him. He has so loved you that He gave His only Son for you, that you might have eternal life, which is surely, irreversibly yours. He has spared not His own Son, but given Him up for you; how shall He not with Him give you all things? Who can accuse you when God will justify you in Christ Jesus? Who can *condemn* you, when Christ has died for you, and is ever at the right hand of God? Neither tribulation, nor distress, nor doubt, nor thoughts which rise against your will, nor power of darkness, nor hell, can separate you from the love of God which is in Christ Jesus our Lord.

"These are not my words, but the words of God Almighty, spoken directly to you in the Scriptures, which you must so believe and follow as that you can laugh at your gloomy thoughts; comforted and joyful in your trust in the Almighty Lord, from whose hand no man can pluck you, follow your calling which He has committed to you. Childlike obedience is the sacrifice well-pleasing to God.

"I cannot, without more certainty than I now have, answer definitely your question, whether it is best for you, in your present condition, to read the *Idea Fidei*.

"I do not know that you are now in a state to comprehend properly a consecutive book upon religious subjects; whether it were not better to give yourself up to reading the Holy Scriptures, alternately with your friends, and talking about it with them. Do not indulge in solitary thought; stir yourself up in the society of pious friends, and talk with them about other than strictly religious matters. Give yourself to the calling which God has intrusted to you. Could you not also be associated with dear Professor Ritter, whose affection for you will surely not fail?

"I am always at your service, gladly, with all that our God gives me.

"I thank you for your undeserved confidence, and once more, with my whole heart, wish for you the blessing of the Lord, who is surely near to you, in as great a measure as you desire—as He is to all who call upon Him with broken hearts.

"With my whole heart, yours,

"NEANDER."

HIS INTEREST IN FOREIGNERS.

Neander's sympathy knew no bounds of nationality and creed. As he was ready to serve every German youth, so had he a warm welcome also for every foreigner who visited him as a theological student, or as a friend of the kingdom of God. In Switzerland, France, England, Scotland, and America there are many worthy ministers still living who have experienced his kindness and hospitality, and hold him in thankful remembrance. Through such visits, where his familiarity with the French and English languages did him excellent service, he scattered noble seed into distant lands, which has since sprung up in quiet stillness, and is now yielding fruit a hundredfold.

For Americans he had a certain partiality, as the freedom of the church and religious life, undisturbed by political influence, fell in specially with his taste. He heartily approved the voluntary principle, the self-support and self-government of the churches, which ruled in the apostolic and ante-Nicene age. He admired the great energy and progress of America, but he often expressed his abhorrence of the institution of slavery, and was at a loss to understand how it could be tolerated and even defended in a free country in this nineteenth century. Nor did he approve of sectarian divisions and distractions; for he was emphatically a man for union, and sought the one in the manifold no less than the manifold in the one.

Among his American pupils was Dr. Edward Robinson, the pioneer of Palestine exploration; and when I first met him in New York, in 1844, with letters of introduction from Neander and Ritter, he said to me:

"Of all men I ever knew, August Neander and Karl
Ritter are the greatest and the best."

Neander's library was transferred to American soil, and
is among the literary treasures of the Baptist Theological
Seminary at Rochester, N. Y.

CHARACTER OF NEANDER.

Neander presented a rare combination of virtues re-
fined by grace. He was truly an *anima candida*, an
Israelite without guile, like Nathanael. He was a legiti-
mate descendent of Abraham, without the cunning and
selfishness of Jacob. He had the noble traits of his
Jewish ancestry, but none of its besetting vices. He
was a Jew in his outward appearance, but a genuine
Christian and nobleman within.

His characteristic traits were simplicity, generosity,
humility, and love.

He presented a striking illustration of the words of
our Lord—" Except ye become like little children, ye
shall not enter the kingdom of heaven." He was truly
a child in malice, though a giant in knowledge. His
spirit lay clear and open before God and men. He had
the simplicity of the dove, without the wisdom of the
serpent. He gave his confidence to everybody, and
could not easily believe an evil report. Hence he was
often deceived. With all his theoretical knowledge of
human nature he was liable to err in the application to
particular persons. As has been said, he knew *man* better than *men*.

We have already spoken of his unselfish devotion to
his students and to all who were in need of his counsel
and help. He had for his own person few wants ; his
clothing was of the plainest sort ; his moderation in eat-

ing and drinking reminded one of the lives of the old
ascetics and of St. Anthony, who felt ashamed of the
need of earthly food. By reason of his impractical nature, moreover, and his total abstraction from the world,
he was indeed wholly ignorant of the value of money,
and had not his sister taken care of it, he would no doubt
have brought himself to beggary over and over again by
sheer benevolence. In this respect he showed not a
trace of his Jewish descent.

Of conjugal love he knew nothing ; and yet how
highly he conceived of the dignity and worth of woman !
How beautifully he has portrayed the influence of pious
mothers upon the character of Gregory Nazianzen,
Chrysostom, and Augustin ! How tenderly devoted was
he toward his sisters, especially to that one who gave
herself up to the care of his earthly wants, that his rich
mind might be consecrated to the undisturbed service of
religion !

This rare character, full of childlike simplicity, tender
conscientiousness, unwearied professional fidelity, and
warm, self-sacrificing love—this life wholly consecrated
to the advancement of truth and piety—was rooted and
secured throughout in the grace of humility. Neander
knew the corruption of human nature, and the necessity
of its redemption in Christ ; placed himself cheerfully in
the great concern of life by the side of the least ; with
all his uncommon learning preferred the simple, unadorned preaching of the gospel for poor sinners to the
most brilliant displays of rhetoric ; listened on Sunday,
with close attention and devotion, to the message of the
foolishness of the cross, which yet puts to shame all the
wisdom of this world ; and with all his popularity and
his world-wide fame never allowed himself to be blinded
by vanity and pride. He remained, to the last breath,

as humble as a child, and would be nothing in himself, but all only in and through Christ. "It is the most difficult of all arts," he says in his beautiful essay on Paul and James, "to deny and to empty one's self, to become nothing in ourselves, in order that we may be all in the Lord alone. In this art we remain pupils through life, but it brings the richest and most glorious fruits for eternity. Oh, that we may exclaim with the Apostle of the Gentiles, 'I have been crucified with Christ; and it is no longer I that liveth, but Christ liveth in me!'" On the last celebration of his birthday, when his students lauded him with their customary enthusiasm, he answered with a touching confession of his sin and weakness and entire dependence on the forgiving mercy of our Saviour. One of his favorite mottoes, which he wrote in my album, was, "*Theologia crucis, non gloriæ;*" and according to this motto he lived till life's frail tenement gave way, and his spirit passed into the full vision of the crucified One in glory.

We must not suppose, however, that Neander was free from human frailty. He had a sensitive and irritable temper, and at times was even intolerant. With all his love and gentleness, he was yet capable also of very strong and decided aversion and indignation. This is by no means unpsychological. Hatred is only inverted love. The same force that draws toward it what is in harmony, repels from it with equal determination what is of a contrary nature. John, the disciple of love, who lay on Jesus' bosom, was at the same time "a son of thunder," and ready to pray down fire from heaven upon the enemies of his Master; yea, according to ancient story, he forsook a public bath suddenly, when he found it contained Cerinthus, the Gnostic heretic. Both sides of his character are reflected in the fourth Gospel and in

the Apocalypse ; the former is full of love and tenderness ; the latter resounds with thunder and lightning. A
similar combination of mildness and harshness, attracting
love and repulsing hatred, was characteristic of Neander.

As an historian he could do justice to the most different tendencies, and took even heretics, as far as possible,
into his protection ; but when kindred manifestations
came before him in our time and in the same University
he showed himself impatient and intolerant, at least in
private conversation. He was often morbidly irritated
and passionately excited about the pantheistic philosophy
of Hegel on the one hand, and the stiff, angular orthodoxy of Hengstenberg on the other. Hegel had died in
1832, but his philosophy was then at the zenith of its
power and influence in Prussia, and represented by Marheineke in the theological faculty. Hengstenberg was
a younger colleague of Neander, and the fearless champion of orthodoxy in the chair and in his writings.
Neander saw in these opposite tendencies two dangerous
extremes, which threatened to rob the youth of Germany
of the treasure of evangelical freedom, which he prized
above all things. From the Hegelian philosophy he
feared the despotism of thought ; from the strict orthodoxy the despotism of the letter. He hated the one-sided
intellectualism and panlogism of the former, the narrow
spirit and harsh judgments of the latter. There Christianity seemed to him to lose itself in the clouds of idealism, here to stiffen into dead formalism. Besides, he
held it altogether vain to seek the restoration by force of
any past period of the Church as such, or to dream of
infusing new life again into that which has been once for
all judged and set aside by the course of history. Yet,
after all, he had a sincere personal regard for Hengstenberg, who stood firm as a rock against the waves of Ra-

tionalism, and who fully reciprocated the esteem of Neander.   He never indulged in personalities, and was
always controlled by pure motives and love for the truth.

The character of Neander was universally esteemed
and admired.   True, he also had decided theological
enemies.   For the Orthodox of the more strict class he was
in many points too lax and liberal ; for the Rationalist,
too positive and firm ; but for his person all entertained
a sort of sacred veneration, and treated him with more
mildness and forbearance than is usual with such difference of views.   Even Strauss, the author of the
mythical theory of the Gospel history, when Neander
came out in strong defence of the genuineness of the
Gospel of John, was led to abandon his doubt for a while
(in the third edition of his *Leben Jesu*, 1837), although
when he saw the fatal consequences of this concession he
returned (in the fourth edition, 1840) to his former
sceptical view.

The reasons for this general esteem are apparent.
Neander's deep and accurate learning were not sufficient
to protect him against the " fury of theologians." What
constituted a tower of strength and made him invulner-
able was his all-controlling love of truth and justice, his
modesty and humility, his moral purity and integrity.
These qualities at once struck even the superficial
observer, and admitted of no doubt, for he always showed
himself as he was, without any concealment or reserva-
tion.   An attack upon his character, an impeachment
of his motives, could have sprung only from stock-blind
passion, would have awakened indignation among those
who knew him, and so must have resulted almost inevi-
tably in the moral discomfiture of the antagonist.

HIS THEOLOGY.

Neander was one of those truly great men with whom theory and practice, head and heart, are beautifully blended. Not without reason had he chosen for his motto : " *Pectus est, quod theologum facit.*" Marheineke and the Hegelians contemptuously called him the *pectoral* theologian. He pursued theology, not as an exercise of the understanding merely, but also as a sacred occupation of the heart, which he felt to be intimately connected with the highest and most solemn interests of man, his eternal welfare and worth.

The living centre and heart's blood of theology was for him faith in Jesus Christ, as the highest revelation of a holy and merciful God, as the fountain of salvation and sanctifying grace for the world. Whatever he found that was really great, noble, good, and true in history he referred, directly or indirectly, to the divine-human person. of the Redeemer, in whom he humbly adored the central sun of all history and the innermost sanctuary of the moral universe.

There are, no doubt, more orthodox theologians than Neander ; some of his views are hazy, and lack clear and sharp outlines ; he was more profound than acute, more comprehensive than definite. He was, to use an Anglican phrase, an evangelical broad-churchman. With all his regard for the symbolical books, he would never confine himself to their measure, and conscientiously refused to sign the Augsburg Confession. But there are few divines in whom doctrine was to the same extent life and power, in whom theoretic conviction had so fully passed over into flesh and blood, in whom the love of Christ and of man glowed with so warm and bright a flame. In this unfeigned, life-breathing piety, which had its root in Christ's person and gospel, and formed the foundation of his theology, lay the irresistible attraction of his lectures for every piously disposed hearer, and the edifying character of all his writings.

While in this practical bent of his theology he sympathized with the pietistic school of Spener and Francke, which asserted just this practical side of religion—the rights of the heart, the necessity of a *theologia regenitorum*, over against a lifeless orthodoxy of the intellect—he was, on the other hand, far removed from pietistic narrowness and bigotry. His extended historical studies had served to enlarge his naturally liberal mind to the most comprehensive catholicity. He never lost his sound and simple sight for the main object—the life of Christ proceeding from a supernatural source—but he thought too highly of this to compress it into the narrow bounds of a human formula, or some single tendency or school. He saw in it rather such an inexhaustible depth of sense, as could be in some degree adequately expressed only in an endless variety of gifts, powers, periods, and nationalities.

What a difference is there not, for example, between an Origen and a Tertullian, a Chrysostom and an Augustin, a Bernard and a Thomas Aquinas, a Luther and a Melanchthon, a Calvin and a Fénelon ; or, when we go back to the Apostolical Church itself, between a Peter and a John, a James and a Paul, a Martha and a Mary ! And yet Neander knew how to trace out and greet with joyous gratitude the same image of Christ variously reflected in all. He had little interest in the secular surroundings and artistic ornaments of church history, but he always moved in the deep, and brought out the internal, spiritual and eternal relations, and traced everywhere the pervading and sanctifying influence of the gospel working upon every variety of temper and constitution.

The wideness of his heart was an essential element in his practical piety. Between it and his studies there existed a relation of reciprocal encouragement and support. Thus was Neander, in the noblest sense, a friend of man, because Christ's friend ; at home in all spheres of His kingdom, the exact impression of evangelical catholicity, and an interpreter of the precious doctrine of the communion of saints, which transcends all limits of time and space, and comprehends all the children of God under the one head—Jesus Christ.

THE LAST BIRTHDAY.

Among the charming features of German and Swiss family life are the annual commemorations of birth, marriage, and other family events.

Neander's birthday was an occasion of great interest to his friends and students. On his last birthday, Hannah, as usual, invited a large company to dinner. There sat at his right hand the court-chaplain Ehrenberg, his favorite preacher ; at his left the philosopher Schelling, who in his old age created a literary sensation in Berlin by his lectures on the Philosophy of Mythology and the Philosophy of Revelation, and broke down the supremacy of Hegel ; there was Prediger Lisco, another of his favorite preachers, the author of *The Parables of Jesus* and a monograph on the *Dies Iræ ;* his colleague, Professor Strauss, the court-chaplain, and friend of his youth ; his other colleague, Dr. Immanuel Nitzsch, a *homo gravis*, and, like him, denominated one of the Church Fathers of the nineteenth century ; Professor Piper, one of his early pupils, and an expert in Christian archæology ; Dr. Trendelenburg, Professor of Philosophy in the University ; Dr. Krummacher, the hero of the German pulpit and author of *Elijah the Tishbite ;* Lachs, the Director of the Deaf and Dumb Institution ; Dr. Julius, an enthusiast for prison reform, after the Pennsylvania system of solitary confinement ; and Director Ranke, brother of the historian. A truly illustrious company ! His friends and colleagues, Dr. Twesten, the successor of Schleiermacher, Leopold Ranke, the historian, and Karl Ritter, the founder of comparative geography, were also usual guests of Neander on such occasions, but I do not find their names on the list of those present at the last birthday dinner.

After dinner followed the customary toasts. The genial Strauss, who excelled in sparkling postprandial speeches, eulogized Neander's *Church History*, but announced the startling news that he was *not* the sole author of it. The guests looked at each other in surprise ; Neander turned on his chair ; Hannah looked indignant, when Strauss continued : " Yes, that work could never have been written without a helpmate, and that helpmate is among us—Hannah Neander, the most devoted of sisters, who relieved him of care and anxiety, that he might wholly devote himself to his calling ; long life to her !" Strauss laughed heartily, the guests shouted applause, and the Neander children looked at each other with a complacent smile.

Toward evening friend after friend, male and female, entered the parlor with hearty congratulations. Suddenly the flickering glare of a torchlight procession was seen in the street, and about a hundred students began to sing, with clear, strong voices : " The Lord is my Shepherd ; I shall not want." A deputation of the students was admitted, and thanked their beloved teacher for continuing his lectures, notwithstanding his bodily infirmity and blindness.   They were forbidden of late to offer him presents of books or ornaments as they had done before, but begged him to accept instead a liberal donation for his " Society for the Relief of Sick Students."   Neander, unable any more, as in former years, to address the serenaders from the window, expressed, with trembling voice, his thanks to his " dear fellow-students and beloved friends," to whose fellowship he owed his youthfulness in old age, and then most heartily shook hands with every one, as they came up by his request from the street, after throwing their torches together in a heap.   The students parted with a good-night by singing,

"*Integer vitæ scelerisque purus.*"

This last birthday of Neander on earth was soon to be followed by the celebration of his first birthday in heaven.

SICKNESS AND DEATH.

Neander had a frail and delicate constitution.   In the last years of his life he became, in a peculiar sense, a theologian of the cross, with the painful experience that the *via lucis* is indeed also a *via crucis.*   He was doomed, like the illustrious author of *Paradise Lost,* to an almost total loss of sight, long before weakened by incessant study.   His faith gave him power to bear this calamity, doubly severe to an historian.   To him might be applied what St. Anthony once said to the blind teacher, Didymus of Alexandria : " Let it not trouble thee to be without the eyes with which even flies can see ; but rejoice rather that thou hast the eyes that angels see with, for the vision of God and His blessed light."   He could say what was said of Milton :

"On my bended knee
I recognize Thy purpose, clearly shown :
My vision Thou hast dimmed, that I might see
Thyself—Thyself alone."

Not a murmur, not a sound of complaint or discontent, passed Neander's lips ; and in this way the crown was set upon his character by patience and quiet resignation to God's will.

He did not suffer himself to be interrupted in his work by this affliction, and showed in it a rare power of will over opposing nature.   Not only did he continue to hold his lectures as before with the most conscientious fidelity, but he went forward unceasingly also in his literary labors, with the help of a reader and amanuensis. Nay, even within a few months of his death he founded, in connection with Dr. Julius Müller, of Halle, and Dr. Nitzsch, of Berlin, a valuable periodical (*Deutsche Zeitschrift für christliche Wissenschaft und christliches Leben*), and furnished for it a number of excellent articles (such as a retrospect of the first half of this century, one on the difference between Hellenic and Christian ethics, another on the practical exposition of the Bible), in which he still soared with unabated strength, like an eagle.

What his departed friend Schleiermacher had wished for himself in his *Monologues*, and afterward actually received, was granted also to Neander, the privilege namely of dying in the full possession of his mental powers and in the midst of his work.   Only eight days before his death, on the occasion of a visit from Gützlaff, who was regarded by many as " the Apostle of the Chinese," he made an address with youthful freshness on the Chinese Mission, and looked hopefully forward to the future triumphs of the kingdom of God, the setting forth of whose growth, under the guidance of the two-fold likeness of the mustard-seed and leaven, he considered the great business of his own life.

On the following Monday, the 8th of July, he delivered his last lecture, in the midst of severe pain from an attack of sickness, so that his voice several times failed, and he was scarcely able with the help of students to come down the steps of the rostrum. But notwithstanding this, immediately after dinner, which he hardly touched, he set himself again to dictating for the last volume of his *Church History*, which was to describe the close of the Middle Ages and the preparation for the Reformation, until exhausted nature fastened him to his bed.

Then he had his last and severest trial to endure, in ceasing to work for the kingdom of his Divine Master, which had always been his life and joy. Several times he wanted to gather himself up again, and became almost impatient when the physician refused to allow it. But his affectionate sister now reminded him of what he used to say to her in sickness, to engage her submission to medical treatment: "It comes from God; therefore must we suit ourselves to it cheerfully." Calmed at once, and as it were ashamed, he replied: "That is true, dear Hannah; it all comes from God, and we must thank Him for it." So formerly St. Chrysostom, whose life and deeds Neander had delighted to portray, expired in banishment with the exclamation: "God be praised for all!"

A few hours before his dissolution, on Saturday afternoon, the modern "Father of Church History" once more collected his sinking strength, and taking up the thread of his unfinished work just where he had left off before, dictated an account of the so-called "Friends of God," those remarkable German Mystics of the fourteenth and fifteenth centuries, who helped to prepare the way for the evangelical Reformation.

After this appropriate conclusion of his literary activity, about half-past nine o'clock, he longed for rest, and in a sort of half dream, as at the end of a toilsome journey, addressed his sister with the significant words : *"I am weary, let us go home!"* When the bed had been put in order for his last slumber, he threw the whole tenderness and affection of his heart once again into a scarcely audible *" Good-night!"*[*]

He slept for four hours, breathing always more softly and slowly ; and with the morning of the Lord's Day, on what is styled in the Christian year the Sunday of Refreshing, he awoke in the morning of eternity among the spirits of the just made perfect.   There in the company of the great and good men of past ages, with whom he was so familiar, he rests from his labors, in adoration of Him who is the beginning and end of all history.

Neander died within a few weeks of several prominent men of his age—a statesman of England, a President of the United States, and a King of France.   He had occupied no ministerial post, like Sir Robert Peel ; had won no laurels of victory on the battle-field, like Presi-

---

[*] There is a slight variation in the reports of his significant farewell words.   Rauh (*Zum Gedächtniss Aug. Neand.*, p. 9) gives them : *" Ich bin müde ; wir wollen uns fertig machen, um nach Hause zu gehen."* Krummacher (p. 25) : *" Ich bin müde ; wir wollen uns fertig machen und nach Hause gehen."*   Strauss (p. 18) : *" Ich bin müde, lass uns nach Hause gehen."*   He omits the words : " Let us get ready."   All agree as to the last word—" Good-night."   Strauss adds : *" Lieber, theurer Freund, wir hören deinen Abschiedsgruss, wir, Deine Schüler, Deine Freunde, Deine Verwandten, Deine verwaiste Schwester.   Wir hören ihn heute auf's Neue und werden ihn bis ans Ende unserer Tage hören ; und wir erwiedern ihn mit unserem betenden : Gute Nacht, das Dich in die Ewigkeit hinüberbegleitet."*

dent Taylor ; had adorned no throne, like Louis Philippe ; and in the loud tumult of worldly life his voice was not heard. But from his lecture-room and solitary study he exercised an influence quite as far-reaching and enduring as that of any of his companions in life and death. His influence was only more deep and beneficent by being inward and spiritual, and will continue to be felt without interruption as long as theologians and ministers of the gospel shall be trained for their heaven-appointed work. Though political history knows nothing of the quiet, humble scholar in Berlin, his name shines but the more illustriously for this in the records of the kingdom of heaven, which will outlast all governments of earth. Though no monument should be raised to him of brass or marble, a far better memorial is already secured to him in the grateful hearts of thousands who have been his hearers, or readers, or who in coming time shall draw from his works a knowledge of the sorrows and joys, the conflicts and triumphs, the all-pervading and transforming power of the Christian religion, as well as from his life the priceless lesson, that all true spiritual and moral greatness roots itself in simplicity, humility, and love.

" The dead are not dead, but alive."

Hannah Neander never recovered from the death of her brother. Her cheerfulness was gone. She walked no more unter den Linden and in the Thiergarten ; she never visited Carlsbad again ; she kept on a widow's mourning, and moved away from the Markgrafenstrasse to a desolate home nearer her brother's grave. There she sat hour after hour with her weary, half-blind eyes fixed upon a bust of Neander. When a friend wished her a happy birthday, she replied : " Don't ! I

L

have no more birthdays, for I have no more life." She died July 2d, 1854.

THE FUNERAL.

Seldom did a death create more genuine sorrow, and a funeral attract more attention in Berlin and throughout Germany than that of Neander.

Dr. Friedrich Strauss, Neander's colleague and the favorite chaplain of King Friedrich Wilhelm IV., delivered an address in the house ; Dr. Friedrich W. Krummacher, the greatest pulpit orator of Germany, spoke at the open grave in the Jerusalem Church-yard ; and Dr. K. Immanuel Nitzsch, Professor of Theology, concluded the solemnities with an address in the Aula of the University before the assembled learning of the metropolis.

Strauss chose for his text the words : " That disciple therefore whom Jesus loved saith unto Peter, It is the Lord" (John 21 : 7). He characterized his departed friend as a genuine disciple of St. John, filled with the love of Christ, who in all the paths of church history traced the miracles of Christ's love, but who also, like the " Son of thunder," kindled in wrath against the enemies of his Master. And truly he was a forerunner of the Johannean love and peace which sooner or later will dawn upon the Church and solve its discords. Krummacher called him " one of the noblest of the noblemen in the kingdom of God, a prince in Zion," of whom it may be said, as of John, " that that disciple should not die." Nitzsch spoke of his merits as an historian who revolutionized church history, and made it a book of devotion as well as instruction, who awakened sympathy for every manifestation of Christ's spirit, and who fully verified the word, " Seek the things that are above where Christ is, and not the things that are upon the earth." " He left," said Nitzsch, " the best example of true greatness based on simplicity and humility—*Have pia anima.*" *

A VISIT TO NEANDER'S GRAVE.

On the 25th of August, 1884, I made, in company with a Lutheran clergyman, Dr. Stuckenberg, then American chaplain in Berlin, a pilgrimage to Neander's grave in the *Alte Jerusalemer Kirchhof.* There he rests between his mother and his sister Hannah. An iron railing surrounds the lot, and a cypress grows on the mortal remains. A marble bust of Neander in relief, erected by his sister, marks his grave, and bears the simple inscription :

AUGUST NEANDER
geb. 16 *Jan.* 1789
gest. 14 *Juli* 1850.
Dem unvergesslichen Bruder
die Schwester.
1 *Cor.* xiii. 12.

The verse referred to was a favorite text, which is added to his picture in the Boston edition of his *Church History :* " Now we see in a mirror, darkly ; but then face to face : now I know in part ; but then shall I know even as also I have been known."

To his right repose the ashes of Neander's mother and married sister, marked by two iron crosses, with the inscription :

---

* *Zum Gedächtniss August Neander's, herausgegeben zum Besten des Neanderschen Krankenvereins,* Berlin (Karl Wiegandt), 1850, pp. 36. This pamphlet contains an account of Neander's last illness by S. Rauh, Lic. theol., and the three funeral addresses of Strauss, Krummacher, and Nitzsch.

Eine edle Frau, eine gute Mutter,
ELEONORE NEANDER,
geb. Frankfurt a. M., Sept. 24 1755,
gest. Berlin, 7 *Juli* 1818.

The name of his married sister :

CAROLINE HENRIETTA SCHOLTZ (1778–1860).

To the left of Neander rests his faithful sister Hannah, who took such good care of him. A marble cross is erected on her grave, and bears the inscription :

JOHANNA NEANDER,
gestorben 2 *Juli* 1854.

On the back—
" *Selig sind, die im Herrn sterben.* "
(" Blessed are those who die in the Lord.")

On the same and the following day, and in company with the same American friend, I visited the graves of Fichte, Hegel (and his wife, who survived him several years),[*] Schleiermacher (and his wife and son Nathanael), Marheineke, Steffens, and other celebrities of the Berlin University. They awakened in me touching reminiscences of the days of my youth ; but none made so deep an impression on my heart as the grave of my beloved teacher and friend, Neander.

---

[*] Hegel died in 1831, nine years before I came to Berlin, but I knew his widow very well. Her maiden name was Marie von Tucher. Her cousin, Mrs. Dr. Tholuck, introduced me to her in 1840. She was an excellent, pious lady, and a friend of Gossner. She was much disturbed by the developments of the radical left wing of Hegel's school (the so-called " Hegelingen"), and the appearance of the infidel *Life of Jesus,* by Strauss ; but she assured me that her husband would have utterly disowned it. She believed him to be a good Christian, though he seldom went to church. He used to make the characteristic excuse ; " *Mein liebes Kind, das Denken ist auch Gottesdienst.* "

I also called on his only surviving colleague, Leopold von Ranke, the greatest living historian, who after publishing many special histories of the highest merit is crowning his life's work, in his ninetieth year (he was born in 1795, six years after his friend Neander), by dictating, with unclouded mind out of the fulness of information, a general history of the world. He gave me a most interesting account of his daily habits and his views on some of the great problems of the age. He is in full sympathy with the evangelical catholic spirit of Neander. I shall not forget his wise words concerning the controlling power of religion in the course of history.

A LETTER OF NEANDER.

For several years (from 1840 to 1844) it was my privilege to enjoy the personal acquaintance of Neander, first as a student, afterward as a teacher in the University. I heard his lectures on modern church history, which were never published. He frequently invited me to dinner with older and wiser men, and I spent many hours in his study. I never left his presence without an impression of his greatness and goodness. It was especially at his recommendation that I received and accepted a call as professor of church history and exegesis from the German Reformed Church in the United States. I never regretted that I followed his advice ; for America has proved to me a second and better fatherland.

It was therefore a natural feeling of gratitude which prompted me to dedicate to him the first German edition of my *History of the Apostolic Church*, which was finished during his life, but not published till after his death. In reply to my request for permission, he wrote to me with trembling hand, when nearly blind, the following letter, which is no doubt one of his last. It shows his kindness of heart, and gives his views on the abortive political convulsions which shook Germany in the closing years of his life.

MEIN THEURER FREUND :

Ich kann Ihnen nur meinen herzlichen Dank sagen für das Zeichen Ihres liebevollen Andenkens, das Sie mir öffentlich geben, und für die Ehre, die Sie mir erweisen wollen, indem ich Ihnen zu Ihrem Werke alle Erleuchtung und Kraft von oben wünsche.

Was Ihr Journal betrifft,* so glaube ich, ich habe etwas von demselben durch Ihre Güte, für die ich herzlich danke, erhalten. Es ist gut, dass Sie mich daran erinnern. Ich kann jetzt leicht etwas vergessen und unbenutzt liegen lassen, da ich nur durch fremde Augen lesen kann, seit zwei Jahren leidend an den Folgen einer auf die Augen zurückgefallenen Gicht.

Ich hatte mir vorgenommen, Ihnen zugleich mit diesem Briefe etwas Neues von mir und meine neuen Auflagen zuzusenden ; aber es ist nun unterblieben, da es sich gerade trifft, dass ich alle Exemplare früher verschenkt habe. Wenn der gnädige Gott mich nicht mit meiner Augenkrankheit heimgesucht hätte, würde ich wohl längst die Freude gehabt haben, meinen neuen Band der Kirchengeschichte bis auf die Reformation, vielleicht die Reformationsgeschichte selbst, Ihnen zusenden zu können.

Was man in dem traurigen Jahre 1848 in unserem armen Vaterlande Freiheit nannte, ist etwas ganz anderes, als was der aus den Blüthen englischer Frömmigkeit stammende Geist in Ihrem Amerika sucht und meint. Es war hier der Kampf zwischen *Atheismus und Christenthum,* zwischen *Vandalismus und ächter Bildung.* Schon vor Jahrzehnden weissagte ich es, dass die Weltweisheit des einseitigen Logismus, des Verstandesfanatismus und der Selbstvergötterung zu diesen Folgen ihrer consequenten Negationen führen müsse, wie durch die Popularisirung derselben geschehen ist. Nicht, als ob diese Weltweisheit allein die Schuld trüge, aber sie war der consequenteste wissenschaftliche Ausdruck des herrschenden Zeitbewusstseins und seiner Richtung. Dabei läugne ich nicht, dass auch wahre Bedürfnisse im Zeitgeiste vorhanden sind, und dass nur durch Befriedigung derselben, welche allein das Evangelium zu gewähren vermag, dauernde Heilung erfolgen kann.

Wir stehen am Rande des Abgrundes, des Untergangs alt-europäischer Bildung, oder an den Grenzen, wo eine neue schöpferische Aera

---

* " Der Deutsche Kirchenfreund," publ. Mercersburg, Pa., 1848–1854.

durch mannigfache Stürme sich anbahnen soll, ein neuer grosser Act
in dem Weltumbildungsprocesse des Christenthums. Wir wollen
von der Gnade des langmüthigen Gottes das Letztere hoffen.

Ihnen den reichsten göttlichen Segen für all die Ihrigen, für Ihren
Beruf und Alles, was der gnädige Gott in Ihre Hände gelegt hat,
wünschend, verbleibe ich

herzlich der Ihrige,

A. NEANDER.

Berlin, den 28sten Oct. 1849.

MY DEAR FRIEND :

I can only return my hearty thanks to you for the testimony you
publicly offer me of your affectionate remembrance, and for the honor
you propose to show me, while I desire for you in your work all
illumination and strength from on high.

As regards your Journal, I believe something of it, through your
kindness, has reached me, for which you have my hearty thanks. It
is well that you have reminded me of it. I may now easily forget
anything, and let it lie unused, as I can read only through other
people's eyes, having suffered for two years past from the consequences of a paralysis settled in my own.

I had intended to send you along with this letter something new of
my publications and new editions ; but it is now omitted, as it just
so happens that all my copies have already been given away. If the
good Lord had not visited me with disease in my eyes, I would
have had the pleasure long since of being able to send you a new
volume of the *Church History* as far as the Reformation, and perhaps
by this time even the *History of the Reformation* itself.

What men called freedom in our poor fatherland, during the
mournful year 1848, is something very different from what is sought
and meant by the spirit which has been born from the best English
piety in your America. It was a conflict here between *atheism and
Christianity*, between *vandalism and true civilization.* Even many
years ago I predicted that the secular wisdom of a one-sided intellectual fanaticism, and self-deification must lead to this proper consequence of its negations, as by their popularization has now come
to pass. Not as though this philosophy alone were in fault, but it
was the most strictly consequent scientific expression of the reigning
spirit of the age and its tendency. Nor will I deny that there are
true wants also at hand in the spirit of the age, and that nothing
short of their satisfaction, which the gospel alone has power to
secure, can bring any lasting relief.

We stand on the brink of an abyss, the downfall of the old European culture, or else on the confines of a new creative era, to be ushered in through manifold storms—another grand act in the world-transforming process of Christianity. From the mercy of a long-suffering God we will hope for the last.

Praying that God's richest blessing may rest on your family, on your work, and all that the merciful God has intrusted to your hands, I remain

Affectionately yours,

A. NEANDER.

Berlin, 28th Oct., 1849.

PRINTED BY BALLANTYNE, HANSON AND CO.
EDINBURGH AND LONDON.

WORKS BY PHILIP SCHAFF, D.D.

CHRIST AND CHRISTIANITY:

Studies in Christology, Creeds and Confessions, Protestanism and
Romanism, Reformation Principles, Sunday Observance,
Religious Freedom, and Christian Union.

Demy 8vo, 10s. 6d.

"The paper on 'Christ His own Witness' is an excellent and comprehensive statement of that one of the grounds of faith which has,
happily, come into exceptional prominence in our own day. Theological students will find two invaluable bits of historical analysis in
'Christ in Theology,' and 'Creeds and Confessions of Faith,' as lucid
as they are brief."—*British Quarterly Review.*

"Students of abstract and applied Christianity will find satisfaction in this book."—*Saturday Review.*

"It is able and scholarly, and animated by a liberal and reverent
spirit. Dr. Schaff's evangelicalism is of the purest and noblest
order."—*Scottish Review.*

"Will be read with interest, and certainly not without profit, by
all who are interested in the controversies of the present day."—
Church Bells.

THE PERSON OF CHRIST:

THE PERFECTION OF HIS HUMANITY VIEWED AS A PROOF OF HIS DIVINITY.

Small crown 8vo, 3s. 6d.

"Scholarly care and accuracy are everywhere manifested."—
Christian.

THROUGH BIBLE LANDS:

A NARRATIVE OF A RECENT TOUR IN EGYPT AND THE HOLY LAND.

With Illustrations. Crown 8vo, 6s.

"An interesting and very instructive volume."—*Leeds Mercury.*

"The subject is so full of interest to Bible students, that such a
volume as this cannot fail to prove very generally acceptable."—*Rock.*

"This is a book which we thoroughly and heartily recommend."—
Christian Progress.

"Dr. Schaff's vein of personal narrative and reflection is very
interesting."—*Clergyman's Magazine.*

RELIGIOUS BIOGRAPHY

PUBLISHED BY

JAMES NISBET & CO.

———◦◦◦———

LIFE OF THE REV. W. LINDSAY ALEXANDER, D.D.
By the Rev. JAMES ROSS. Crown 8vo, 7s. 6d.

MEMORIALS OF THE LATE FRANCES RIDLEY
HAVERGAL. By her Sister, MARIA V. G. HAVERGAL. With
Portrait and other Illustrations. Crown 8vo, 6s. Cheap Edition,
crown 8vo, 1s. 6d. ; roan, 3s. ; paper cover, 6d.

FRANCES RIDLEY HAVERGAL—THE LAST WEEK
78th Thousand. 6d. ; paper cover, 2d.

LETTERS OF FRANCES RIDLEY HAVERGAL. Hitherto
Unpublished. Edited by her Sister, MARIA V. G. HAVERGAL.
Crown 8vo, 5s.

LIFE AND LETTERS OF THE LATE REV. ADOLPHE
MONOD, Pastor of the Reformed Church of France. By one of
his DAUGHTERS. With Portrait. Crown 8vo, 6s.

SAMUEL GOBAT, Bishop of Jerusalem ; His Life and
Work. A Biographical Sketch, drawn chiefly from his own
Journals. Translated and Edited by Mrs. PEREIRA. With Por-
trait and Illustrations. Crown 8vo, 7s. 6d.

THE LIFE OF JOHN GORDON OF PARKHILL AND PIT-
LURG. By his WIDOW. With Portrait. New and Cheaper
Edition, crown 8vo, 3s. 6d.

MEMOIR OF CAPTAIN P. W. STEPHENS, R.N., late of
H.M.S. *Thetis.* By B. A. HEYWOOD, M.A. Camb. With Portrait and other Illustrations. Crown 8vo, 6s.

CHOSEN, CHASTENED, CROWNED: A Memoir of
MARY SHEKELTON. With Portrait. Crown 8vo, 3s. 6d.

"A most appropriate gift-book for an invalid."—*Record.*

THE FIRST EARL CAIRNS: Brief Memories of HUGH
M'CALMONT, First Earl Cairns. By Miss MARSH. Sixth Thousand. Crown 8vo, 1s.

BY THE SAME AUTHOR.

MEMORIALS OF CAPTAIN HEDLEY VICARS, 97TH
REGIMENT. With Portrait. Small crown 8vo, 3s. 6d. Also a
Cheaper Edition, 1s. 6d. ; paper cover, 6d.

LIFE OF THE REV. DR. MARSH, LATE RECTOR OF
BEDDINGTON. With Portrait and other Illustrations. Post 8vo,
10s. Cheaper Edition, crown 8vo, 3s. 6d.

THE LIFE OF ARTHUR VANDELEUR, MAJOR, ROYAL
ARTILLERY. Crown 8vo, 3s. 6d.

THE VICTORY WON: A Brief Memorial of the Last Days
of G. R. Crown 8vo, 1s. 6d.; paper cover, 6d.

ARCHIBALD CAMPBELL TAIT: A Sketch of the Public
Life of the late Archbishop of Canterbury. By A. C. BICKLEY.
Second Edition. Crown 8vo, 2s. 6d.

AUTOBIOGRAPHY OF THE REV. WILLIAM ARNOT,
Minister of Free St. Peter's Church, Glasgow, and afterwards of
the Free High Church, Edinburgh ; and a MEMOIR by his
Daughter, Mrs. A. FLEMING. Post 8vo, 9s.

THE LIFE OF THE LATE JAMES HAMILTON, D.D.,
F.L.S. By the Rev. WILLIAM ARNOT. With Portrait. Post
8vo, 7s. 6d.

A BIOGRAPHICAL SKETCH OF SIR HENRY HAVE-
LOCK, K.C.B. By the Rev. WILLIAM BROCK, D.D. With
Portrait. Crown 8vo, 3s. 6d. Cheaper Edition, 1s 6d.

A MEMOIR OF THE LATE REV. W. II. HEWITSON, OF
DIRLETON. By the Rev. JOHN BAILLIE, D.D. With Portrait.
Crown 8vo, 5s. Cheaper Edition, 1s. 6d.

BY THE SAME AUTHOR.

A MEMOIR OF ADELAIDE L. NEWTON. With Portrait. Crown 8vo, 5s. Cheaper Edition, 2s.

MEMOIR OF THE LATE REV. WILLIAM C. BURNS,
M.A., Missionary to China. By the late Professor ISLAY BURNS,
D.D., Glasgow. With Portrait. Small crown 8vo, 3s. 6d.

" William Burns is one of the few men of modern times who have carried
the Christian idea into such active revelation in the life as would compel,
even from the most sceptical, a reluctant consent to the Divine orgin of the
truths he taught and lived by ; and his memoir, written with rare sincerity
and simplicity, must long live as a bright specimen of true Christian biography."—*Contemporary Review.*

THE STORY OF COMMANDER ALLEN GARDINER,
R.N. With Sketches of Missionary Work in South America.
By JOHN W. MARSH, M.A., and the Right Rev. the BISHOP of
the FALKLAND ISLANDS. With Portrait and Maps. Crown
8vo, 2s.

MEMORIALS OF JAMES HENDERSON, M.D., F.R.C.S.,
Edinburgh, Medical Missionary to China. With Portrait. Crown
8vo, 3s. 6d. Cheap Abridged Edition, 16mo, 1s.

MEMOIR OF THE LATE REV. J. J. WEITBRECHT, late
Missionary of the C.M.S. in Bengal. Compiled by his WIDOW
from his Journal and his Letters. With a Preface by the late
Rev. H. VENN, M.A. Crown 8vo, 3s. 6d.

SEED-TIME IN KASHMIR: A Memoir of WILLIAM J.
ELMSLIE, M.D., F.R.C.S.E., late Medical Missionary of the
C.M.S. in Kashmir. By his WIDOW and Dr. W. BURNS THOM-
SON, Medical Missionary. Crown 8vo, 4s. 6d. Cheaper Edi-
tion, 1s.

PASSAGES IN THE LIFE OF AN INDIAN MER-
CHANT: Being Memorials of ROBERT BROWN, late of Bombay.
Compiled by his Sister, HELEN COLVIN. Crown 8vo, 5s. 6d.

MEMORIALS OF LITTLE NONY: A Biography of NONY HEYWOOD, who was the First Collector for the Bruey Branch of the Irish Society. By her MOTHER. With Preface by Miss HAVERGAL, and a Portrait. Crown 8vo, 2s. 6d.

"The great charm of the book is its unmistakable reality."—*Churchman.*

MEMORIALS OF A QUIET MINISTRY: Being the Life and Letters of the Rev. ANDREW MILROY. By his Son, the Rev. ANDREW WALLACE MILROY, M.A. Oxon. With Portrait and other Illustrations. Crown 8vo, 3s. 6d.

MEMOIR OF THE REV. G. T. DODDS, OF PARIS. By Rev. HORATIUS BONAR, D.D. Crown 8vo, 6s.

SELECT REMAINS OF ISLAY BURNS, D.D., of the Free Church College, Glasgow. Edited by the Rev. JAMES C. BURNS. With a Memoir by the Rev. W. G. BLAIKIE, D.D., New College, Edinburgh. Post 8vo, 7s. 6d.

MEMORIALS OF A CONSECRATED LIFE. By the Rev. WILLIAM LANDELS, D.D. Small crown 8vo, 3s.

MEMORIALS OF AGNES ELIZABETH JONES. By her SISTER. With Portrait. Crown 8vo, 3s. 6d.

JOYFUL SERVICE: A Sketch of the Life and Work of EMILY STREATFIELD. By her SISTER. Crown 8vo, 1s.

A MISSIONARY OF THE APOSTOLIC SCHOOL: Being the Life of Dr. JUDSON, Missionary to Burmah. Revised and Edited by HORATIUS BONAR, D.D. Crown 8vo, 3s. 6d.

THE LITTLE BUGLER OF KASSASSIN. By Mrs. BALLARD. Square 16mo, 2s. Cheap Edition, paper cover, 1d.

MEMOIR OF ELIZABETH FRY. Abridged from the Larger Work. By her Daughter, Mrs. CRESSWELL. With Portrait. Crown 8vo, 3s. 6d.

MEMOIRS OF CHARLES A. CHASTEL DE BOINVILLE.
Compiled from his Journals and Letters. By the late THOMAS
CONSTABLE, Author of "Archibald Constable and his Literary
Correspondents." Crown 8vo, 6s.

A LIFE OF CONSECRATION : Memorials of Mrs. MARY
LEGGE. By one of her SONS. Crown 8vo, 8s. 6d.

THE LIFE AND LETTERS OF ELIZABETH, LAST
DUCHESS OF GORDON. By the Rev. A. MOODY STUART,
D.D., Author of "The Bible True to Itself," &c. With Portrait.
Small crown 8vo, 3s. 6d.

LETTERS OF RUTH BRYAN. Edited by the Author of
"Handfuls of Purpose." With a Preface by the Rev. A. MOODY
STUART, D.D. Crown 8vo, 5s.

CONFLICT AND VICTORY : The Autobiography of the
Author of "The Sinner's Friend." Edited by the Rev. NEWMAN
HALL, LL.B. Crown 8vo, 2s. 6d.

A BRIGHT LIFE. By Mrs. MACKENZIE. With Portrait
on Steel. Crown 8vo, 3s. 6d.

A NARRATIVE OF SOME OF THE LORD'S DEALINGS
WITH GEORGE MULLER. Written by HIMSELF. Parts I.,
II., and III., price 3s. 6d. each. Part IV., 2s. 6d. Part V., 3s. 6d.

LIFE AND LABOURS OF GEORGE MULLER. 16mo, 1s.

LETTERS SELECTED FROM THE CORRESPONDENCE
OF HELEN PLUMPTRE, Author of "Scripture Stories," &c.
Third Edition. Crown 8vo, 3s. 6d.

THE STAR-LIT CROWN : A Short Sketch of the Last
Illness of the Rev. G. ALBERT ROGERS, M.A. 16mo, 1s.

LIFE OF MRS. STEWART SANDEMAN, OF BONSKEID
AND SPRINGLAND. By Mrs. G. F. BARBOUR, Author of "The
Way Home." Crown 8vo, 6s.

MEMOIR OF CAPTAIN M. M. HAMMOND, late of the Rifle Brigade. Crown 8vo, 5s. Cheap Edition, 1s. 6d.

MEMOIR OF CAPTAIN H. E. HARINGTON, V.C., late of H.M. Bengal Artillery. 16mo, 6d.

A MEMOIR OF JOHN LOVERING COOKE, formerly Gunner in the Royal Artillery, and late Lay Agent of the British Sailors' Institute, Boulogne. With a Sketch of the Indian Mutiny. By the Rev. C. H. H. WRIGHT, B.D. Crown 8vo, 3s.

LIFE AND LETTERS OF A SOLDIER. By Mrs. EVERED POOLE. 16mo, 1s. 6d.

MEMOIR OF ROLAND LAMBERT. Small crown 8vo, 1s., paper cover ; 1s. 6d., cloth ; 2s., cloth, gilt edges.

THE NIGHT LAMP : A Narrative of the Means by which Spiritual Darkness was Dispelled from the Deathbed of AGNES MAXWELL MACFARLANE. By the late Rev. JOHN MACFARLANE, LL.D. With Portrait. Crown 8vo, 3s. 6d.

LIFE OF MRS. COLIN VALENTINE. By Mrs. GEORGE CUPPLES. Crown 8vo, 3s. 6d.

MEMOIR OF THOMAS WILLS. By his Mother, MARY WILLS PHILLIPS, and her Friend, J. LUKE. With Portrait. Crown 8vo, 3s. 6d.

"Scarcely any book would it be so wise to place in the hands of a youth with a passion for science as this. It will stimulate to work, it will guide in moral character, and it will also tell him when to stop."—*Nonconformist.*

THE OFFICER'S DAUGHTER : A Memoir of Mrs. ELIZABETH TATTON. To which are added some Instances of Divine Grace in the Army. By OCTAVIUS WINSLOW, D.D. Fcap. 8vo, 2s. 6d.

A GOLDEN SUNSET : Being an Account of the Last Days of HANNAH BROOMFIELD. By the Rev. J. R. MACDUFF, D.D. 16mo, 1s.

LONDON : JAMES NISBET & CO., 21 BERNERS STREET, W.